MIRROR

AWAKENING

Written by
Dario. M. Gardiner

Table of Contents

Acknowledgements

First, I would like to thank God almighty for making this all possible, for giving me this story to share, for blessing me with the talent and capability to write this novel. I also want to thank God almighty for being with me every step of the way, for giving me this dream, and for giving me the strength and will to complete this novel to the end.

I would like to express my gratitude to the many people who saw me through this book; your support, patience and belief in me made this novel what it is today.

I would like to thank my family, especially my dad, my mom, and my brothers. I would also like to thank my friends, along with my family for their encouragement and for their undying faith in my ability and dream, to complete this novel despite the challenges.

A very special thank you goes out to a very special lady by the name of Frederica Sturrup. Composing this novel was a journey in itself and I can boldly say, because of this wonderful woman's support, constant encouragement, patience and belief in me, I was able to complete this book. Thank you, Frederica!

I would like to thank my editor. I want to thank K and T Graphics for their amazing artwork and design of this novel's cover. I would also like to thank Amazon for publishing this book and for making the process easy to publish a novel.

Last, but not least, a very special thank you goes to you, my readers. Not only for your patronage but also for choosing and giving this novel and I, a chance to entertain and fill you with awe, as it is my mission...

To bring fantasy to life, add depth to originality and put a twist on reality.

Prologue

Falling victim to the constructs of her mind, an eight-year-old girl stares blissfully into the abyss of a large mirror as she fantasizes about being a princess. Engulfed in her imagination, the eight-year-old stands proudly in her plum colored frill dress, exhibiting the acclaimed royal pose. With a hug and kiss, her father walks in and smiles as he unites in her regal aspirations. After sharing a tender moment with his beloved daughter, he helps her put on her coat then leads her outside to a white sedan.

Kissing her goodbye, the father puts his eight-year-old daughter into the vehicle and closes the car door gently behind her then watches as the vehicle departs. Now en route to her destination, the eight-year-old looks back and observes a mysterious black SUV turning into her driveway. With his back turned the father re-enters his home and grabs his black overcoat. Oblivious to the present danger that surrounds him, the father prepares for a routine day, as he is unaware of the three-armed men dressed in black that exits their vehicle and infiltrates his home.

With a strong sense of awareness that he was not alone, the father turns around only to meet his fate as the trio opens fire on him. Propelled backwards by the force of the bullets, the father collides into the mirror, causing it to tip over and fall on top of him as his body drops to the floor.

Then an ominous presence fills the air as a dark man walks inside, brandishing a chrome Beretta dressed in a designer suit. Flipping the mirror over, the men from the SUV roll the father onto his back then the man in the suit points his gun and recites his signature end quote. Lying face up on top of the mirror the father gasps his last breath and slowly stutters a prayer as he accepts his fate, then with the pull of the trigger, the fatal shot was delivered.

Caleb & Eric
{20years Later}

If history has taught us anything, it has taught us that the spirit of competition has reigned in the hearts of men since the beginning of time. As life would have it, another rivalry is born as two opposites, Caleb and Eric, compete for the highly coveted position of Sales and Marketing Assistant Director at Global Media advertising agency. With the opening of the position a decree has been issued to management stating, "The title of Assistant

Director for Sales and Marketing will be awarded to the manager who can come up with the most innovative marketing strategy that will make G.M. the leading marketing firm in the country, and in turn increase our market share which will increase profits."

Popular amongst his peers and ever so confident, the braggart Eric begins to boast that he was the one receiving the promotion and that the announcement was nothing more than a mere formality, until one afternoon at work he accidentally overhears a private conversation between Caleb and his girlfriend Andrea. As Eric continues to listen, he becomes aware of Caleb's brilliant marketing strategy that would not only meet the company's goal but exceed all expectations. After eavesdropping on Caleb's conversation and assimilating his plan, Eric is troubled as self-doubt begins to invade the confines of his mind as he thinks to himself, *If Caleb gets that promotion over me, I'll be a laughingstock and I won't be able to show my face. I can't let that happen.* Fueled with jealousy and envy, Eric decides to steal Caleb's portfolio.

Later that evening with the intent to carry out his deceitful plan, Eric shrewdly sneaks into Mr. Blackwell's secretary's file cabinet and switches the names on both his and Caleb's portfolios. Meanwhile down the hall, Caleb deliberately meets up with Mr. Blackwell, as he is en route to his office and invokes a moment of his time. Abrupt in manner, Mr. Blackwell replies "Make it quick" but before Caleb could utter a single word, both he and Mr. Blackwell, unexpectedly catch Eric in the file cabinet with a gray portfolio in his hand. Caught off guard, Eric pitches up and says, "Mr. Blackwell, I didn't expect to see you, sir!" Skeptical as to why Eric was in his secretary's file cabinet, Mr. Blackwell looks at the portfolio in his hand and asks, "Is that for me?"

"Yes," Eric stutters. In hearing his response, Caleb quickly tries to rectify the situation and attempts to speak up, but Mr. Blackwell cuts him off and says, "You had your time." Then Mr. Blackwell motions to Eric for him to hand over the portfolio.

With guilt written all over his face as Mr. Blackwell skims through the marketing proposal, Eric begins to sweat profusely as he nervously looks at Caleb, hoping to get away with his deceit. In an effort to right the wrong done to him and expose Eric's treachery, Caleb tries to speak up but his righteous indignation was thwarted once again by Mr. Blackwell as he dismisses him and shakes Eric's hand saying, "This proposal is amazing."

"Thank you, Mr. Blackwell." says Eric as he smiles, modestly.

"Eric, don't be bashful, this proposal is genius; you just guaranteed yourself the promotion. Congratulations," exclaims Mr. Blackwell. Then inviting Caleb into the conversation, Mr. Blackwell turns to him and says, "Caleb, come congratulate Mr. Jameson, he's your new boss and our new Sales and Marketing Assistant Director," Forced by circumstance, Caleb unwillingly shakes Eric's hand and congratulates him.

CHAPTER: I

The Meeting

Days later, stretched out on a chaise lounge Caleb finds himself talking to a psychiatrist, telling her everything that has been going on at work with him and Eric. He explains to her how Eric constantly disrespects him, how he undermines his authority and his most recent unethical behavior, the theft of his marketing proposal and unworthy acquisition of what should be his promotion. Astonished by what she heard, the psychiatrist looks at Caleb and asked, "Did you talk to your boss about this or even confront Eric about what he did?"

"No," Caleb sighed.

"Then why tell me?" replied the psychiatrist.

As Caleb's silence confirms her professional intuition, the psychiatrist readies her prognosis and said,

"I'll tell you why, it's because deep down this situation is still bothering you and you know, you need to resolve this." Still reluctant to deal with the issue, Caleb puts both hands over his face and sighed, then the psychiatrist said, "It's unhealthy and unnatural for you to have all these unresolved issues bottled up inside you. These unresolved issues can lead to a nervous breakdown or even worse, you could possibly develop a split personality and heaven forbid..." Just then, before the psychiatrist could finish her statement, Caleb's mobile phone goes off and immediately he jumps up and exclaimed, "I have to go. We'll have to finish this some other time." Then quickly gathering his things, Caleb grabs his coat and scampers out of the psychiatrist's office.

Thirty minutes later, Caleb makes his arrival at an Italian bistro named Angelo's, where he had a lunch date planned with his girlfriend, Andrea. Upon entering the restaurant, Andrea welcomes Caleb with a big hug and kiss, expressing her melodramatic happiness on seeing him. "Congratulations honey! I'm so proud of you," she said. Doing his best to play it off, Caleb shrugs his shoulders and smiles sheepishly. With a big smile on her face Andrea said, "Honey, this is your moment; you deserve this. No need to be bashful, I already knows you got the promotion. Mr. Blackwell couldn't stop talking about your marketing strategy." Then taking Andrea's hands and holding them tightly, Caleb exclaimed, "I didn't get it."

"Caleb, what are you talking about? Mr. Blackwell just released the new marketing strategy for the company, the same strategy you shared with me," Andrea said as she rose from the table.

"Andrea, I didn't get the promotion," exclaimed Caleb.

Then with his head down, Caleb breaks the news and explains how Eric stole his portfolio and gave it to Mr. Blackwell as his own and that Eric was the one receiving the promotion and not him. But firm in his belief, that good will always prevail over evil, Caleb said, "Don't worry, people like Eric always gets theirs in the end."

Infuriated by Caleb's lackadaisical attitude, Andrea lashes out at him and scolds him sternly, "I can't believe you're letting Eric get away with stealing your idea and taking your promotion and you're not doing anything about it. You are weak and pathetic. You will never amount to anything because you always let people walk all over you!"

After expressing her disgust, Andrea storms out of the restaurant and leaves Caleb humiliated and alone. Taking a taxi back to the office, Caleb goes to Andrea's office hoping to smooth things over with her, but as he approaches her office, he notices that her office door is slightly open. Carefully approaching the door, Caleb peeks his way through and to his surprise, he gets the shock of his life as he sees the unimaginable: Eric and Andrea kissing and groping before his very eyes. Consumed with rage, Caleb pushes the door wide open and startles the lip-locking duo as he glares at Andrea then storms out of her office. Walking angrily down the hall, Caleb bumps into Eric's secretary, Sophie, causing her to drop all of her paper work. Without a shred of care or remorse Caleb doesn't even stop to say "sorry," he just keeps walking until he finally exits the building.

After walking a few blocks away to clear his mind, Caleb finds himself in front of an antique store, mesmerized by a large wall size mirror that catches his attention. Gazing into the mirror, Caleb becomes petrified as a sinister reflection of himself appears. Freaked out by his menacing reflection, Caleb turns away in fear: afraid of the realization that the psychiatrist's prognosis was coming true. After gathering his thoughts, Caleb takes a second look, to confirm what he saw and in doing so he notices that his evil mirror double had vanished. Relieved that his evil mirror twin had disappeared, Caleb quickly departs from the antique store and makes his way home.

CHAPTER: II

Belac Is Released

The next day, after a night of getting very little sleep, Caleb strolls to work tormented and hurt as he is haunted by the daunting visions of Eric and Andrea kissing. Struggling to find some kind of peace, Caleb tries to put everything that happened behind him but like a song being replayed, Caleb is reminded by the words of his psychiatrist as her voice plays back in his mind. "It's unhealthy and unnatural for you to have all these unresolved issues bottled up inside you. These unresolved issues can lead to a nervous breakdown or even worst, you could possibly develop a split personality." At that moment, almost instantaneously the vision of his sinister reflection rises to the fore-front of his mind.

While continuing on his journey, Caleb is exonerated from his captivating thoughts as he is joined by his close friend and adviser Phillip. And as the two meet along the way, Phillip takes a keen observation of Caleb's appearance and exclaimed, "Rough night?"

"Is it that noticeable?" asked Caleb.

"Pretty much but no big deal, it happens. Hey! Before I forget, I got you a self-help book; it should arrive any day now. It's designed to help you reach your Edge," said Phillip.

"Thanks, Phil, I could use all the help I can get," replied Caleb.

"Kay, talk to me. What's going on?" asked Phillip.

"I'll tell you in the elevator," exclaimed Caleb.

After selecting their respective floors, Caleb reveals the heart-breaking truth about Eric's promotion and of Andrea's infidelity. Sucking his teeth in disgust Phillip exclaims, "Eric is one conniving asshole! Kay, you can't let him get away with this, you have to tell Mr. Blackwell the truth: that promotion is rightfully yours. As for that harlot, I told you before she's an opportunist. Andrea is just looking for any opportunity to move up." Repulsed by Phillip's callous remarks about Andrea, Caleb turns away and continues the rest of the elevator ride in silence. As the elevator stops on the tenth floor, Phillip exclaimed, "Kay, think about what I said, I'll catch up with you later." After his one on one with Phillip, Caleb exits the elevator on the 15th floor feeling worse than he did before. Walking only a few steps into the hallway Caleb observes Eric brandishing a brand new suit. Burning with resentment, Caleb watches Eric, like a hawk watches its prey, as he roams the hall receiving congratulatory remarks for his topnotch marketing strategy then all of a sudden while fixated on Eric, a mandatory manager's meeting was announced.

Throughout the course of the meeting, Mr. Blackwell spoke about the legacy of G.M. and the new direction that the company will now be going in, thanks to the new marketing strategies that will be implemented. Upon nearing the end of his address, Mr. Blackwell proclaimed, "I have an announcement to make; Eric can you please stand up." Continuing on Mr. Blackwell says, "Now as you all know, we were looking for a new Assistant Director for Sales and Marketing. We were looking for someone who would not only assist in keeping G.M. on the cutting edge but will also make Global Media the leading advertising agency in the country. So we offered the position and issued a challenge to any manager interested to apply. Many came forward but only one was chosen and we have made our decision. Ladies and Gentlemen, I present to you, Eric Jamison, our new Assistant Director for Sales and Marketing." While everyone is clapping and congratulating Eric, a Senior Marketing Director leans over and says to Caleb, "I know you were really gunning for that promotion and I'm sorry you didn't get it, but right now I expect your support more than the others as Eric transitions into his new role as Assistant Director.

After the conclusion of the meeting, Caleb quickly exits the boardroom and goes into the kitchen for a drink of water as he tries to suppress his discontentment. Then all of a sudden, while Caleb is consuming a bottle of water, Nick enters the kitchen and purposely bumps into him, causing Caleb to choke and spill his water. To make matters worse on top of feeling like a fool, Caleb now felt like a peon as Nick brushes off the incident like it was nothing and said, "Relax, it's not like you're going to drown," he laughed as walked away. More upset than he originally was Caleb hurtles his way out of the kitchen and crashes into Eric's secretary. However, this time was different, instead of leaving her there to "pick up the pieces," Caleb helps Sophie up and apologizes for bumping into for a second time.

"It's OK, I know it was an accident" said Sophie as she blushed timidly.

"Again, I'm truly sorry and thank you for being so understanding," replied Caleb.

After helping Sophie and apologizing to her, Caleb attempts to leave the scene when Sophie stops him and boldly asked if he had been to lunch. In response to her question Caleb replied, "No, I haven't, I just want to catch some air." Seizing the moment, Sophie continues her quest as she invokes Caleb to let her tag along. "Hey, you look like you could use a friend; you mind if I tag along? Before you say no, I know where there is a hot dog stand not too far away, where we could get a bite to eat and also get some fresh air at the same time." Thinking about his relationship, Caleb starts to turn down Sophie's appeal to join him, but after the unspeakable vision of Eric and Andrea smooching renewed itself, he changes his mind and replied, "You know what, that sounds like a good idea. Come on, let's go."

After walking three minutes in complete silence, Sophie decides to open the lines of communication and asked, "Is everything OK?" Without giving him a moment to respond, Sophie continued and said, "I noticed the last couple of days you haven't been yourself." Then like water from a broken dam and feeling like the weight of the world was on his shoulders, Caleb breaks his silence and reveals the truth about Eric's promotion and Andrea's betrayal. Sympathizing with his plight Sophie exclaimed, "Sometimes, life can be so unfair, if it makes you feel any better, I think you'd make a better assistant director than Eric." Sophie smiled. Smiling back Caleb replied, "It does, thanks...come on let's get those hot dogs." After getting their hotdogs, Caleb said, "Hey Sophie, there's an antique store a block away from here, I want to check out. I saw something in the window that caught my attention and I wanted to see if it's still there." Overwhelmed with insurmountable joy to have extended alone time with Caleb, Sophie willingly agrees to his request and exclaimed, "What are you waiting for, lead the way."

As they approach the antique store, Caleb looks into the display window and notices that the mirror wasn't there. Sucking his teeth, he said, "It's not there, let's go."

"What isn't there?" asked Sophie curiously.

"The mirror that I saw there yesterday... but it's gone now. We can head back to the office, it's no big deal." exclaimed Caleb.

"You give up way too easy. Let's check inside, they may have just moved it," replied Sophie.

Going into the antique store, Sophie pushes the door open and shouted, "Hello?"

"Good day! How can I help you?" asked the store clerk.

"Hi, my friend saw a mirror in your display window and we were wondering what happened to it?" Then joining the petition, Caleb cleared his throat and said, "Yesterday there was a large wall size mirror in the display window that caught my attention and I just wanted to know if you still have it?" asked Caleb.

"Oh yes that one, we moved it to the back. If you go through that aisle, all the way to the back you will find it." answered The clerk with a smile.

After receiving information on the whereabouts of the mirror, Caleb and Sophie continue their quest as they stroll towards the back of the antique store. As the two persist to the back of the store, Caleb catches glimpse of the mirror and taps Sophie on the shoulder and exclaimed. "There it is." As Sophie looks at the gold framed wall size mirror, she drops her soda and screamed, "Oh my God!" repeatedly. Quickly turning to her, Caleb interrogates Sophie for her reason for screaming as he ponders if she too, had seen his sinister reflection. Readying himself,

Caleb prepares mentally to face his evil counterpart but before he could do so, Sophie shouted, "That's my daddy's mirror. I can't believe it, I used to always dress up and pretend that I was a princess while staring in it." With a sigh of relief, Caleb exhales, then Sophie declared, "Caleb, I have to have this mirror, no matter the cost!" Without giving Caleb a chance to utter a single word, Sophie hurries off to inquire about the mirror. In a low-pitched voice, Caleb replied, "I'll be right here... just looking around." With a battle raging in his mind, Caleb contemplates if he should look into the mirror and face his ominous double or forget about what he saw completely. Finally making up his mind to do so, Caleb decides to get it over with and look in the mirror. To his surprise, he looks into the mirror and sees only his reflection and after repeated trials of looking again and again, he becomes comfortable with the idea that his evil mirror double had vanished for good as he thinks to himself, *Maybe it was just my imagination.* Feeling confident that all was well and that he had nothing to worry about, Caleb takes a final look into the mirror, then all of a sudden, he receives the shock of his life as he comes face to face once again with his sinister mirror reflection. Petrified and intrigued at the same time, Caleb moves closer to the mirror and examines it. Then it happened like a flash of lightning, Caleb's reflection grabs him and pulls him into the mirror, trapping him inside the glass prison cell while simultaneously makes his escape. Now the sinister mirror image, Belac is released.

CHAPTER: III

Difference

Liberated from his mirrored prison cell, Belac looks around and says, "Freedom at last." Then staring into the mirror he fixes his clothes and says to Caleb, "I'm working this side of the mirror." Oblivious to the events that had taken place, Sophie returns from her transaction, unaware of the substitution that was made and walks up to Belac and exclaims, "Wow!" as she takes note of his appearance. Examining him more closely, Sophie says, "There's something different about you, I'm not sure what, but I think this mirror has something to do with it," she smiled. With a confident smirk, Belac replies, "You have no idea." Then observing the clock on a wall and realizing that their lunchtime was up, Sophie exclaims, "Caleb! It's time for us to go; we have to get back to the office."

Now on their journey back to the office, calamity nearly strikes as a boy riding a bicycle dashes past them and almost crashes into Belac. In a fit of rage Belac lashes out at the boy, "Watch where you are going, you little asshole!" he shouted angrily. Dumbfounded by his out of character behavior, Sophie stares at Belac with amazement and thinks to herself, *What's gotten into Caleb? I've never seen him act like this before. He must be blowing off some steam.*

After the incident had occurred and they were back at the office, Sophie smiled and said,

"It was nice having lunch with you today, Caleb."

"It was, wasn't it? We should do it again, some other time," replied Belac as they casually stroll past Andrea's office. Then hearing Caleb's response and disbelieving what her ears heard, Andrea ponders to herself, *I wonder who that is Caleb is talking to?* With, cat-like reflexes Andrea rush towards the door to see with her own eyes, who Caleb was talking to and have her question answered. Stunned by his appearance, Andrea's eyes widen as she gaze upon Belac with great desire. Then focusing her attention on the mystery woman that is walking with Belac, jealousy and envy reared their ugly heads, as Andrea identifies the mystery woman to be none other than Sophie.

The next morning as Belac prepares for his day at the office, he takes careful time selecting the best suit in his closet. After choosing a suit of his liking, he meticulously goes over the choice suit with an iron, ensuring that there were no imperfections. Further prepping as a part of a man's morning ritual; Belac polishes his shoes, takes a warm shower and shaves. After getting dressed and taking the necessary grooming steps to safeguard his immaculate appearance, Belac departs for work. Later with his arrival, Belac is unexpectedly joined by Phillip, who runs over to meet him, just before he enters the elevator. Taking a moment to catch his breath, Phillip looks at Belac and offered an apology.

"Kay, I'm sorry for what I said about Andrea yesterday, I shouldn't off have talked about her like that."

"Hey, forget about it; you only spoke, what was needed to be said," exclaimed Belac. With a stun look on his face, as the elevator opens Phillip stares at Belac and thinks to himself, *After all this, all it took was a book*. Then he smiled and exits the elevator.

Moments later with his arrival on the 15th floor, Belac steps out of the elevator and instantly a cloud of silence fills the room as he walks through the office. Then all of a sudden with great admiration for his stylish apparel, Belac is bombarded with a series of nonstop compliments. As the day goes on, reports of Caleb's new appearance spreads like wildfire, until finally it reaches the ears of Andrea. After hearing all the buzz about Caleb's new look, Andrea makes plans to visit the new and improved Caleb as she decides it's time to reclaim what's rightfully hers. Meanwhile proceeding to his office, Sophie greets Belac in the hall way and engages him in conversation as she compliments him on his bold new look.

"Good morning, Caleb, you look very handsome today," said Sophie sheepishly.

"Good morning, thanks. You look quite lovely yourself," replied Belac.

Surprised by his flirtatious response Sophie blushes uncontrollably as she relished the rare tender moment. As their friendship begins to blossom in what seems to be the start of something new, here comes Eric on cue, like a plague; disrupting the serenity of harmony.

"Sophie, I need you to file these documents, ASAP," exclaimed Eric.

"Yes, right away, Mr. Jameson. Caleb, I'll see you later," replied Sophie.

Watching her leave, Eric said, "Caleb, I see you finally got yourself a decent suit; it's about time. I'll be honest it is a nice suit, but on me…" Quickly stopping him in his tracks before he could finish his monologue, Belac shouted, "Eric, go to hell! Your days of stealing from me, are over." With the bold accusation, that Eric removed his belongings without his permission; an awkward silence fills the office. Then rejecting the claim and pretending like he didn't know what Belac was talking about, Eric daringly asked, "What are you referring to?" With fire in his eyes, Belac replied, "You really want me to answer that?" Terrified that the truth about his ascension to assistant director would be revealed, Eric humbles himself and turns away then Belac whispered, "I thought so," and walks off. With all eyes on him, Eric for the first time found himself on the receiving side of humiliation and as the murmurs got louder he shouted, "Everyone back to work!" then retreats to his office.

After all this happened, Andrea confides in a girlfriend and says to her, "Cover for me, I'm going over to see Caleb." Skillful in the art of seduction, Andrea preps, like a hunter before the hunt; powdering her nose, spraying on sweet perfume, hiking up her skirt and lotioning her legs. With her agenda in play, Andrea walks to Caleb's office and boldly let's herself in. With the looks of a goddess and the body of a vixen, Andrea does her best to entice Belac with her provocative behavior, but it was all in vain. Annoyed by her attempts to seduce him, Belac interrogates Andrea and asked, "What do you want, Andrea? Why are you in my office?" With a bewitching smile Andrea replied, "Why do I need a reason to see my man?" Irritated by Andrea's response Belac squints his eyes, as he watches her play with a pencil on his desk and exclaimed, "I don't have time for this, please go." Ashamed and rejected, Andrea softly answered, "I only wanted to make things right between us."

After being ousted by Belac, Andrea exits the office, feeling like a fool as she closes the door behind her. While in the process of departing from Caleb's office, Andrea catches a glimpse of Sophie's head quickly turning as she is about to leave. Indignant about Sophie's apparent spying, Andrea decides to walk over and have a chit-chat with Sophie to mark her territory. "Sophitia, were you spying on us?" asked Andrea. Intimidated by Andrea's confrontational style, Sophie replied, "I heard loud talking coming from Caleb's office and I was a little concerned, that's all, I wasn't spying."

"You were concern, for who?" asked Andrea, then she said, "Let me tell you something, Sophitia, don't think for one second that you will ever get between me and Caleb. He's just having a hard time dealing with being passed up for that promotion, that's all; but as soon as this blows over, things will be back to normal. So stay far away from my man; got it?" Nodding her head, Sophie replied, "Got it."

Meanwhile in his office, Belac receives a phone call from Mike, the mailroom guy, who informs him that a package came in for him and that he needs to come down and collect it. After agreeing to pick up his package, Belac hangs up the phone and leaves for the mailroom. Determined to get in Belac's good grace, Andrea secretly watches him go, then decides to sneak into his office and leave him a memento. After gaining access inside Caleb's office, Andrea tiptoes around and proceeds to put her underwear in his top drawer, but too her surprise as she was about to place her undies in the drawer, she notices a paper on the desk with Eric's name written on it.

With his arrival at the mailroom, Belac walks through the doors and straight up to the counter and says, "I'm here for my package." With his back turned and no sense of urgency, Mike looks back at Belac then throws a book on the counter and says, "Your package." Aggravated by Mike's callous attitude and by the grievous appearance of his newly acquired book, Belac stares longingly at his mangled paperback book, then questions Mike about the conditions of his book. Laughing out loud, in response to Belac's question, Mike replies, "If a miracle can't help you, what in the hell makes you think this book can." After making sport of him and sobering up, Mike informs Belac that he needs to sign the release form, to verify that he had received his book. Going into the cabinet, Mike bends down to retrieve the release forms, and as he searches through the cabinet, Belac picks up a box cutter off the counter top and with an angry look on his face, he walks slowly behind Mike. Squinting his eyes, Belac brutally slashes Mike repeatedly down his spine. After butchering Mike, Belac hides his body under a table, and flings the box cutter under a chair and turns off the light.

While the misdeed of murder was being perpetrated, Andrea takes the paper off the desk and quickly makes her escape. Returning to his office, calm as a summer's breeze, Belac reclines at his desk quite relaxed. Then all of a sudden, Belac notices that the paper he left on his desk was missing. Infuriated that the paper was gone, Belac frantically searches for the missing document drawer by drawer. After failing to find the missing document and coming to the realization that someone had taken it, Belac turns his exploration outward. Opening his office door with the force like that of a hurricane wind, Belac shouts, "Who the fuck was in my office!" In total shock, everyone freezes and looks around as they wondered, "What was going on". Hearing about the commotion that Belac was making over the paper that she took, Andrea sits in her office quiet and afraid, hoping that no one saw her enter or leave his office. Continuing his loud outcry, Belac shouts, "Who in the hell was in my office and moved a document off my desk. I want it back now!" Hearing Belac's vicious uproar, Eric shouts, "Caleb, in my office now!"

CHAPTER: IV

The Dream

Furious with Belac for his loud outburst and use of explicit language, Eric takes a deep breath as the door closes then directs Belac to have a seat. Still in a hostile mood, Belac refuses the invite and opts to remain standing. Then testing the waters Eric exclaims, "Ever since I got this promotion you have been acting quite different. Your behavior and attitude has changed considerably, as if you were someone else. What's going on with you?" asked Eric. Refusing to participate in Eric's mind game, Belac ignores Eric's question and stands there quietly staring at him. Annoyed by Belac's silence and blatant disrespect towards him, Eric shouts, "Oh! I see now you don't have anything to say, but just a minute ago you were out there carrying on like you own the damn place. Caleb, I think you better lay off the suits; it's getting to your attitude. So let me put things back in perspective: I am the boss, not you, Caleb. You will do as I say and you will act accordingly. You don't raise your voice or throw a tantrum up here. If there is an issue, you come to me and I will deal with the situation. Do I make myself clear?" Then with a menacing look on his face, Belac opens the door then looks back and says before leaving, "Yes Eric, you are in charge; but I promise you, not for long."

Now that his day at the office had come to an end, Belac returns to his apartment and retires for the evening. Later that night as he sleeps comfortably in his bed, Belac begins tossing and turning repeatedly. As he tossed and turned, Belac starts breathing heavily as he tugs on his blanket and clinches his eyes. Then a vision descends upon him and Belac finds himself down on his back, staring at the barrel of a gun, struggling to breathe. Surrounded by thugs dressed in black, all except one, Belac mumbles his last words. With the gun pointed at its target the shooter tightens his grip, and makes his final declaration then seconds later, boom, the gun goes off and Belac immediately wakes up, rattled and gasping for air. Turning his attention to the alarm clock, Belac looks the time and sees that it is 10:50 p.m. Without thinking he jumps out of bed and runs to the closet, quickly putting on dark colored clothing and takes off mysteriously into the night. With a mean look on his face, Belac walks a few blocks away, until finally he stops at an old-fashioned bar and lounge called Moon-lite. With boldness and familiarity, Belac goes into the lounge and pulls out a barstool then beckons for the bartender. After two minutes of waiting with no one in sight, Belac becomes impatient and starts banging on the bar counter, yelling "bartender." About thirty seconds later, a distinguished gentleman comes from the back and asks, "What are you having?" Belac answers, "I'll have a Manhattan cocktail, with Canadian whiskey, an ounce of vermouth and a dash of Angostura bitters, stirred in a glass with ice and I would like an olive." With a peculiar look on his face the bartender looks at Belac and says,

"I haven't heard anyone order this particular drink in about 20 years." After exchanging a few casual words with each other, Belac leads the bartender into an inquisition. "So tell me about that guy who used to order this same drink."

"Well, he was a tough looking guy with a unique personality and he wasn't a big talker. You kind of remind me of him: same drink and same kind of face." After hearing the bartender's comparison of himself and the anonymous male, who favored the same drink, Belac boldly asks the bartender if he knew where he could find a man by the name of Gerard.

With his eyes widened and senses heightened the bartender freezes at the mere mention of Gerard's name and cancels making the signature mix drink, then instructs Belac to leave immediately. But based on the bartender's reaction and stern mandate for him to leave, Belac quickly deduces that the bartender was hiding the fact that he actually knew Gerard and that he was being very disingenuous. Belac cleverly asks to have his drink. With an unfavorable look, the bartender reluctantly agrees to finish make the signature mix drink then proceeds to give Belac his beverage. In a sequence of events as it relates to what happened next, Belac quickly takes his alcoholic beverage, then using a modified disarming maneuver he takes control of the bartender's hand, twisting his middle and ring fingers together as he slammed his head on the counter and interrogates him. "Start talking, where I can find Gerard?" Belac asked forcefully. In agonizing pain the bartender exclaimed, "I told you, I don't know anyone named Gerard."

"Wrong answer" replied Belac.

Then grossly applying pressure to the bartender's hand, Belac breaks the bartender's fingers, sending the broken bones protruding through the palm of his hand. In a loud voice the bartender shouts, "Fuck!" Without any kind of remorse, Belac continues his interrogation as he urges the bartender to tell him the truth with threats of more physical harm. "You better tell the truth, before I really get angry and break more than these two fingers," exclaimed Belac. Unable to bear the excruciating pain, the bartender defects and screamed out, "Ok, shit! Every Friday night just before midnight, one of Gerard's guys comes in and has a few drinks then leaves about two o'clock. That's all I know, I swear." Satisfied with the information that he received, Belac releases the bartender, and picks up his drink and guzzles it down, then exclaims, "Ahh! You haven't lost your touch." After consuming his drink, Belac opens his wallet and puts a twenty- dollar bill on the counter then tells the bartender to keep the change and leaves.

CHAPTER: V

Death at the Office

Beep! Beep! Beep! Awakened by the buzzing sound of the ringing alarm clock, Belac struggles to open his eyes as he fights to disable the sounding alarm. After silencing the alarm, Belac rubs his eyes to view the time, then in disbelief that it was eight o'clock, he sighs, "Morning already." Puzzled as to why he was so tired, Belac drags himself out of bed and strolls to the bathroom. Peering into the mirror, Belac becomes dumbfounded as he notices the clothes that he has on and the blood splatter on his shirt. As things continue to get more bizarre, Belac all of a sudden catches the scent of whiskey on his breath. Completely baffled by his appearance and by the smell of alcohol on his breath, Belac exclaims, "What the fuck!" as he is momentarily confused. Unsure of what to make of his current state of being, Belac just ignores the matter and gets ready for work then leaves.

After getting over his morning of weirdness, Belac finally reaches his destination. Upon his arrival, Belac notices five police vehicles and a coroner's van parked in front of the building. As Belac makes his way inside a police officer stops him as he tries to enter the building and asks to see his identification. Annoyed by the officer's request to see his I.D, Belac squints his eyes as he looks at the officer with contempt; then suddenly out of nowhere, Mr. Blackwell's assistant shouts, "It's Ok! Let him through." After the momentary delay, Mr. Blackwell's assistant explains to Belac that there was an incident and that an emergency meeting has been called and that he is expected to attend the meeting in the executive boardroom.

"What's going on?" asked Belac.

"Mike, the mailroom guy, was found dead this morning in the mailroom, he was murdered." replied Mr. Blackwell's assistant.

Without emotion or any kind of remorse, Belac says, "How tragic." Then he enters the elevator. Disembarking on the 15th floor, Belac steps out the elevator and makes his way to the executive boardroom. While en route to the boardroom, Belac meets Sophie in the hallway, who urges him to make haste.

"Caleb hurry. The meeting just started; it's going to be a long meeting."

"Thanks." replied Belac sarcastically as he enters the executive boardroom.

With one meeting unfolding and another in the employee lounge beginning, Phillip finds himself in the middle of an interrogation as the prime suspect involving the murder of Mike, the mailroom guy. As the interrogation commences, police detectives Granger and Storr both express their uneasy suspicion regarding Phillip and the unusual likelihood of finding a mangled book near a victim's body that resembles the way he was killed. "Mr. Kelly, a book was found near Mikel's dead body, and not just any book but a self-improvement book that you ordered. During our investigation, we were intrigued to find out, that the same book that you ordered was found at the crime scene. And strangely enough it was sliced down the spine, just like Mike." exclaimed Detective Granger.

"Sounds a little too coincidental for me, especially since the box cutter that was used to cut up the book you ordered is the same box cutter used to murder Mike." said Detective Storr. In a state of panic, Phillip shouted, "Wait a minute; you think I killed Mike! That's absurd. I didn't kill Mike! I'm innocent; I had nothing to do with his murder." Slamming his hand down on the table Detective Storr shouted, "The book that you ordered was found at the crime scene, dammit!"

"Yes! I did" exclaimed Phillip.

"So you admit it; you killed Mikel?" asked Detective Granger.

With both detectives in his face, Philip replied, "Mike was a jerk, his attitude sucked and although I didn't care for him; I swear I didn't kill him. Yes, I did order that book, but it was not for me; I got it for a friend."

"A convenient story, you seriously want us to believe that you ordered a self-improvement book for a friend?" asked Detective Granger.

"I know it sounds strange, but I bought that book for my friend Caleb," exclaimed Phillip.

In great disbelief of Phillip's statement, both detectives look at each other, then Phillip says, "Caleb is my best friend and until recently he was going through a real rough time and he needed some help, so when I came across that book 12 Steps to a Better You, I had to order it. Sneering at him, Detective Storr exclaimed, "Tell us more about Caleb and why you had to buy this book for him?" Then Phillip said, "A couple days ago, Caleb was passed up for a promotion and on top of that, he lost girlfriend right after. Caleb is a good guy but he lacked confidence and he always allowed people to get the better of him."

"You're a good friend," replied Detective Storr.

"Like I said, Caleb is my best friend" exclaimed Phillip. Then in a low-key voice he continued, "Caleb always looked to me for advice, so it's not unusual for me to go out of my way to help him. So when I ordered that book the timing was perfect, because the same time it arrived he was going through those problems. It was fate or so I thought. Yesterday, I met up with him at the elevator and I couldn't believe my eyes. Caleb was smooth, he was confident and he was dressed really well. It was like watching Dr. Jekyll and Mr. Hyde, I thought he had gotten the book, but to my surprise, he didn't. When I mentioned the book to him, he didn't know what I was talking about, I can't explain it but Caleb wasn't Caleb."

Now back at the meeting inside the executive boardroom, Mr. Blackwell addressed some of the major issues that G.M. could possibly be facing, as a direct result of the murder of Mike. As Mr. Blackwell spoke about the future of G.M, a look of despair comes on his face as the possibility of losing his company, overwhelms him. Then clearing his throat Mr. Blackwell announces a 15-minute recess. In succession to the announcement of the break, many of the meeting attendees choose the option to leave the boardroom and enjoy the benefit of a break, while the others, including Belac, choose to do the opposite. Unaffected by all the gloom and doom reports and counter scenarios, Belac remained calm and stayed seated until he saw Nick.

As Nick walks past the boardroom, he unknowingly evokes the wrath of Belac as he strolls through the hallway. With an angry look on his face, Belac squints his eyes and exits the boardroom. Going into the office kitchen, Belac blocks the drain with a dishcloth and fills the sink with water then advances to lure Nick into the kitchen. Moving forward with his plan, Belac goes into the refrigerator and takes out a cold 12 oz. can of beer. Then as Nick walks by the kitchen, Belac shrewdly opens the malt beverage and entices Nick as he offers him a beer. Taking a sip, Belac exclaims, "Ahhh, that's good." then hearing Belac's enjoyment of the alcoholic beverage, Nick finds his way into the kitchen. With the trap set and the bait taken, Belac smiles.

"Hey! There's one more left in the fridge if you want it," exclaimed Belac.

"Hell yeah, thanks Caleb, good looking out," replied Nick.

With great delight, Nick goes into the refrigerator, not paying attention to Belac as he proceeds to acquire the prized alcoholic beverage. Pleased that all was going according to plan, Belac gently sets his beer down on the counter then rolls up his sleeves and discreetly locks the kitchen door. With his back turned, rummaging through the refrigerator, Nick cried,

"Hey Caleb, where's the beer, I don't see it?"

"Look on the bottom shelf, in the back," answered Belac.

Frustrated and disappointed because he didn't find any beer, Nick slams the refrigerator door and shouts, "There is no damn beer in this refrigerator!" and begins to mouth off at Belac. But before Nick was able to express his vexation, Belac punches him in the stomach, grabs his head and shoves it into the sink. After violently drowning Nick, Belac drags Nick's lifeless body into the cleaning closet of the kitchen and says, "You were right, I didn't drown. But you did." Then Belac closed the closet door.

Concealing his deadly assault on Nick, Belac mops the floor, unclogs the drain and wipes down the counter then exits the kitchen, closing the door behind him. Attempting to flee the scene of the crime, Belac proceeds to leave the area, when all of a sudden, he is accosted by Andrea.

"Honey, I was just looking for you; I wanted to talk to you about a proposition, I have for you. Can you spear me a minute?" asked Andrea.

"I have to get back to the meeting. What do you want?" Belac said angrily.

Showing her sexual interest, Andrea throws her arms around Belac and smiled,

"I just wanted to tell you, that I have a romantic weekend getaway planned for just the two of us and we won't have to leave our room or even see the sun. Now tell me, how does that sound?" Intrigued with the idea of a weekend rendezvous, Belac replied,

"With an offer like that, how can I refuse?"

"You couldn't, so after the meeting, we'll discuss the details, ok?" Andrea exclaimed as she smiled excitedly. Nodding his head with approval, Belac agrees to Andrea's terms then he and Andrea walk to the boardroom. After escorting Belac to his meeting, Andrea kisses him and walks slowly past Sophie's desk then looks back at Sophie and smiggles as she enters the elevator. About twenty minutes later, going into the second half of the crisis meeting, the boardroom doors abruptly opens as Detectives Granger and Storr, enter the boardroom like armed gunmen.

"What is the meaning of this? This is a private meeting!" shouted Mr. Blackwell. Then Detective Granger said, "There's been another murder."

CHAPTER: VI

Reoccurring Dream

With the proclamation of another murder, the meeting comes to a halt as news of Nick's death, breeds confusion and pandemonium throughout the boardroom. In total disbelief of what he just heard, Mr. Blackwell drops into his chair and cries, "Another murder," as he holds his head, feeling hopeless. Then like one of the twelve, Belac boldly asked, "How did he die?"

"Well we're not sure how yet. But when we found him, his shirt was wet and his hair was damp and frizzy, like he just came out of a pool; either that or he had a massive heart attack, which causes extensive sweating, but I doubt that was the cause of death. However, we will have more to report once the autopsy is complete," answered Detective Storr. Then Detective Granger exclaimed, "But we are ninety-nine percent sure that this man was murdered."

"If you're not one hundred percent sure how he died, how can you classify this as a murder?" asked Mr. Blackwell. Biting his lip and rubbing his chin Detective Granger answered, "Mr. Blackwell, I've been on the police force for over fifteen years and I have never seen anyone, who died from natural causes or from an illness, go in a closet and hide themselves like they don't want to be found then lie down and die. So it's evident that somebody placed the victim's body in that closet to conceal whatever malicious act he or she committed."

"But the killer was sure smart," exclaimed Detective Storr.

"Why do you say that?" asked Belac.

"Because the killer put the victim's body into the kitchen closet where everyone in this room and staff on this floor frequent, so dusting for finger prints is a waste of time and the kitchen was clean,." replied Detective Storr.

"So, what now?" asked another manager.

"Now we need to get a statement from everyone here; so if anyone has any plans, you better make new ones. It's going to be a long day," answered Detective Granger.

Later that evening after a long day of inquests and consecutive meetings, Belac finally arrives home, drained and mentally exhausted. Upon entering his apartment, Belac throws his keys onto the counter top then throws himself down on the couch and falls asleep. Suddenly the telephone rings and Belac's five minute snooze is interrupted as his eyes barely open. Then answering the phone he exclaimed, "Hello."

Immediately with a tone of desperation in his voice, Phillip said, "Caleb! Thank God, you're home. You wouldn't believe what those detectives are trying to do to me!"

"What?" asked Belac

"They're trying to pin Mike's murder on me. Caleb, I swear I didn't kill Mike," declared Phillip.

"Why do they think you had something to do with Mike's death?" asked Belac.

"Remember that book, I ordered for you? They found it at the scene of the crime," answered Phillip.

"Phil don't sweat it; if they had any real evidence, you would have been behind bars by now," exclaimed Belac.

"I guess you're right." Phillip sighed. Then chuckling he said, "It's funny how things change; I remember when you used to call me for advice. Now it's the other way around, Thanks Kay."

"What are friends for... Anyway Phil, we'll talk tomorrow," exclaimed Belac. Then he said, "Good night," and hangs up the phone. As fatigue begins to set in, Belac staggers to the bedroom and flops down onto the bed and falls into a deep sleep.

Later that night as he slumbered in his bed, Belac begins tossing and turning, then all of a sudden a black SUV pulls into the driveway as he makes his way inside. After entering his residence, he walks to the closet and puts on a black overcoat. Quickly turning around as he sensed that he was not alone; he comes face to face with three familiar gunmen, who open fire on him. As the echoing sounds of gunshots fill the air, he drops to the floor as hot lead pierces his flesh and streams of blood gush from his body. Then looking up as he struggles to breathe, he prepares for the end. Troubled by the nightmarish vision of being executed, Belac awakens panic-stricken; drenched in sweat, breathing heavy and looking around then he exclaims, "One more day."

CHAPTER: VII

Philip Arrested

The next morning rising from his slumber, feeling rested and fully energized Belac awakens ready to take on the day. Rummaging through the closet, searching for the right attire to wear, Belac searches diligently for a suit but not just any suit, a suit that would not only announce his presence but would simultaneously make a statement. "Yes, this one will do," he exclaimed, as he comes across the perfect three-piece suit that not only caught his eye, but displayed power. Impressed with the charcoal gray suit, Belac quickly gets dressed and leaves for work.

Now at the office, as everyone is getting along and engaging in their various conversations, Belac steps out the elevator and instantly all eyes were on him. In a brief moment of awe the chatter stops, as the facial expressions of his colleagues exhibit their admiration for his sense of style. Exuding his confidence and feeding off his fellow co-workers' adoration, Belac casually walks through the hallway with a smirk on his face. Then all of a sudden, someone shouts, "Looking good, Caleb." Then the fanfare commences, but only for a short while as Eric makes his presence known. With the scene set for the perfect storm, a cold chill fills the air as Belac's and Eric's eyes meet. As tensions rise, silence takes the office by surprise as everyone anxiously watches Eric and Belac stare at each other. Then metaphorically firing the first shot, Eric said, "Caleb, I need that report from the Accounts Department and bring it to my desk, ASAP." Then pushing past Belac and intentionally bumping into him, Eric whispered in his ear, "It's not the suit that makes you look ridiculous. It's the fact that you thought putting that suit on, would make you feel important does." Eric snickered as he proceeded to walk away. Then all of a sudden, much to Eric's surprise, Belac grabs his arm and pulls him into his shoulder and says, "If I were you I would update my wardrobe and get a black suit; you never know when you may need one." Then pulling his arm away, Eric clears his throat, fixed his necktie and walks away.

"What was that about?" Andrea asked as she walks up to Belac.

"Nothing," replied Belac

"Caleb, I hope you didn't forget about our plans this weekend," Andrea said seductively.

"Remind me again," exclaimed Belac.

"Our weekend getaway," Andrea said as she held his hand and moved closer to him.

"Yes, I remember now." Belac smiled.

"Good," replied Andrea. Then she said, "So here is your key to the room and this key is for the rental car that I got for you. It's the blue Impala, parked under the tree at the rear of the parking lot."

"You thought of everything," exclaimed Belac.

"Yes I did, and you will be surprised to know what else I thought of." Andrea smirked.

Looking at her lustfully, Belac takes the keys then Andrea said, "I will see you Saturday."

"I'll be there," exclaimed Belac with a smile.

Then realizing that Sophie was secretly watching from across the hall, Andrea decides to put on a little show and tips to the top of her toes and pulls Belac into her chest and kisses him very passionately on the lips. After publicly displaying her affection for Belac, Andrea says loudly, "There is more where that came from." Then walking off with a smile on her face, Andrea looks at Sophie and grins as she goes into the elevator then waves goodbye to Sophie.

Totally disgusted by Andrea, Sophie rolls her eyes and says to herself, Bitch!

"Don't let her bother you," exclaimed Belac as he walked past Sophie's desk.

"She doesn't," replied Sophie in a soft voice.

Meanwhile in the employee lounge, Phillip is on the telephone having a conversation with his father, telling him everything that had transpired and how he is a prime murder suspect. "Phillip, you turned your back on me and on the family business and now that you're in trouble with the police, you want my help," exclaimed Phillip's father.

"Dad, please," Phillip replied. Then taking a deep breath, he said, "I know you're disappointed that I never joined the business, but please understand, that's not the life for me." Suddenly the lounge door opens and Detectives Granger and Storr walk inside boldly, as they asked "Who are you talking to?"

"Phillip, don't tell them who you are talking to, you'll only make things worse," declared his father.

"A friend," answered Phillip nervously. After Phillip answered them, a uniformed police officer enters the lounge and withdraws his handcuffs. "Phillip Kelly, we are placing you under arrest for the murder of Mikel Artest and Nicholas Sheffield," exclaimed Detective Granger. As the officer walks over to Phillip, he starts screaming and shouting, "You're making a mistake! I didn't do it!" Then Phillip begins to cry and continues his plea, "I didn't do it!"

"If you didn't do it, who did?" asked Detective Storr. Taking a short breath Phillip shouted, "I don't know but it wasn't me, I swear." Signaling the officer to arrest Phillip, Detective Storr gives the go ahead with a head nod to take Phillip into custody, while Detective Granger reads Phillip his rights.

Entering the employee's lounge, Sophie walks inside and is stunned to see Phillip in police custody and asked, "What's going on?" Detective Storr replies "Phillip is under arrest for the murder of Mikel Artest and Nicholas Sheffield."

"There must be some kind of mistake," exclaimed Sophie.

"There is no mistake; we have evidence linking Phillip to both murders. Now excuse us," replied Detective Storr.

Still hesitant to move, Sophie blocks the doorway then Detective Granger sternly warns her, if she doesn't move out of the way, she would find herself under arrest for obstruction of justice. Moving out of the way, Sophie watches helplessly as the officers escort Phillip through the door and off to jail. After witnessing Phillip being carried off, Sophie throws herself against the wall and begins crying as she drops to the floor.

CHAPTER: VIII

Past & Present Friends

Quietly contemplating in his office, Belac sits at his desk, meditating as he leans back in his chair with an aggravated look on his face. Closing his eyes for a brief moment, mental pictures of getting rid of a certain someone begin to consume his mind. Two minutes later after being bombarded with malicious thoughts, Belac rises up and ruggedly opens the top drawer and grabs a ballpoint pen. Then squeezing the pen tightly in his hand, Belac clicks the pen's trigger and releases the tip. With an angry look on his face, Belac squints his eyes and exits his office. Hiding the pen behind his back, Belac makes his way to Eric's office with one goal in mind. Intently walking towards Eric's office, Belac briefly stops at Sophie's desk, and says, "Hold all of Mr. Jameson's calls and reschedule all of his meetings. He and I have some issues that I need to take a stab at." Then continuing to Eric's office, Belac approaches the door, turns the doorknob and enters quietly.

Engaging in a telephone conversation and relaxing in his leather chair, Eric reclines comfortably with his back facing door and is totally unaware of Belac walking towards him. Then like a fierce storm surge, Belac rushes towards Eric, to deliver the fated deathblow and rid himself of Eric's existence once and for all. Spinning the chair around with one hand stretched back ready to dispatch his ill intentions, Belac willfully drives the ballpoint pen savagely towards Eric's chest. Then suddenly the door opens and a voice shouts, "Caleb, wake up!" Disoriented and stunned, opening his eyes Belac looks up and to his surprise; Eric is standing over him, asking for the Accounts Department reports. "I was just going for it," replied Belac. Then proceeding to leave, Eric stops in the doorway and said, "Perhaps in your dream." Annoyed by Eric's sarcastic remark, Belac looks at him and replied, "You have no idea." Then he gets up and pushes past Eric.

Tormented and torn between reality and what he thought to be Eric's death, Belac storms towards the elevator upset as he makes his way to the Accounts Department. Just then, the elevator door opens and out comes Sophie running towards him, crying and panicking. "They took him," she cried. Caleb! The police... they took Phillip." Quickly taking hold of Sophie and doing his best to comfort her, Belac tells Sophie to calm down and assures her that everything is going to be all right. Taking Sophie to a quiet room to console her, Belac explains the bail hearing procedures as it relates to it being, Friday the weekend. After getting Sophie to realize Phillip's dilemma, Belac says, "Sophie, the only thing we can do for Phillip now is prepare for Monday and pool our resources. So if he makes bail, we'll be able to get him out. In the meanwhile I'll get in contact with his dad; you know he has connections." Wiping her nose and sniffling, Sophie nods her head in agreement and says, "Ok" Then Belac hugs Sophie and tells her he has to go and that they will catch up on Monday.

Later that night, filled with anticipation, Belac gets dressed and puts on a black coat then exits his apartment and drives off in his newly acquired Impala. Moments later, Belac pulls up at the Moon-lite Lounge and parks across the street, patiently waiting for Gerard's guy to show. As time passed on, Belac's patience begins to wear thin as he grows weary, waiting for the mystery man to show up. Just then as Belac s about to call it a night and give up his manhunt, the mystery man finally makes his appearance and enters the lounge. With his patience rewarded, the moment Belac had been waiting for had finally come, as he nods his head and rubs his hands anxiously waiting for the mystery man to exit the lounge. With time progressing slowly, Belac falls asleep as his eyes get heavy and he relives a past life.

Driving along in a two door Cadillac Fleetwood, Belac and his accomplice pull up to a small house. Upon exiting the vehicle, Belac and his associate, the mystery man, start a friendly banter as they walk into the yard. "Hey, do you want the front or the back?" asked the mystery man.

"I'll take the back," answered Belac, then he walks around to the rear of the house. Meanwhile at the front door, the mystery man knocks on the door, then a voice from the inside exclaimed "Who is it?" Not answering the question, the mystery man shouted, "This isn't a social call; where's the boss's money?"

"Tell Gerard, I need a couple more days; I'll pay him

next week," shouted the man from inside. Suddenly as he was making his plea to pay the money owed at a later date, in comes Belac from behind exclaiming, "Wrong answer". Filled with terror, the man turns around and to his surprise, standing there ready to attack was the infamous I.C. "Wait!!!" shouted the man as he begs for mercy, but it was too late. The job was carried out with a thunderous blow to the face, the deadbeat drops. Finishing his ruthless assault on the deadbeat for not paying his debt, Belac breaks the man's jaw, arm and six of his ribs. Upon leaving the home, Belac warns him, "I'll be back next week and you better have the money or I will break your legs." Then he shuts the front door as he leaves. Walking back to the car, his partner said, "I don't even want to know."

"I wasn't going to tell," replied Belac. ,

"That's why you're the best; you have no emotion or care. You just do what you have to do." said his partner as he smiled to himself.

"It's just business, no feelings needed...now let's go," replied Belac.

"Drinks are on me," exclaimed his one-time friend as they drove off.

CHAPTER: IX

The Rendezvous

Awakening from his brief nap, Belac opens his eyes just in the nick of time to catch his former colleague, exiting the lounge and going into a black sedan. Carefully following his former comrade at a watchable distance, Belac drives slowly behind, hoping to obtain valuable information on the whereabouts of Gerard. After driving for a while Belac's one-time friend now foe, glances into his rear view mirror again and notices the same blue Impala that was a couple cars behind him, is still behind him. With his suspicion heightened, Belac's former colleague, speeds up and takes an unexpected turn and watches to see if the blue sedan would follow. With his eyes glued to the rear view mirror, Belac's former partner anxiously waits for the blue Impala to turn the same corner to confirm his gut feeling of being followed.

Then it happens, the blue Impala diverts through the same corner, thus confirming his suspicion. At that moment, Belac's former brother in arms slams the gas pedal and speeds off in fear, not knowing who was on his tail. Aware that he had been discovered, Belac races behind his ex-partner in hot pursuit. Blazing up and down the street, corner after corner, Belac and his former comrade's high speed chase suddenly turns chaotic, when Belac's former colleague produces a hand gun and starts firing shots at him. Conscious that it would be unwise to continue the pursuit in this manner, especially being unarmed, Belac decides to discontinue his chase and makes a tactical retreat. Noticing that the Impala had stop following him and changed direction, Belac's ex-partner perceives that the driver of the blue Impala had given up the chase. Ensuring that no one was following him, Belac's former ally stops his vehicle and double checks his mirrors and the surrounding area, assuring that the blue Impala was nowhere in sight. After confirming that it was safe to continue his journey, Belac's former co-conspirator drives off. Then all of a sudden, moments later while Belac's ex-partner crosses an intersection, a bright light blinds him as the sound of a blaring horn catches him off guard and to his amazement, the blue Impala rams into his car, sending him and the vehicle, flipping across the street.

Wasting no time at all, Belac quickly gets out of his vehicle and runs over to the wreckage and pulls his former colleague out of his car and begins interrogating him. "Hey, I'm looking for Gerard, tell me where I can find him?" asked Belac.

"Screw you! I'm not telling you a damn thing, exclaimed his former colleague.

"Wrong answer," replied Belac.

Furious with his former colleague's response, Belac balls his fist and unloads a series of punches on his one-time friend then questions him again. "Where can I find Gerard?" Belac asked forcefully.

"What business do you have with Gerard?" asked his former comrade.

"Unfinished business," replied Belac. Then taking a couple of short breaths his former colleague said, "You're a dead man walking and you don't even know it. Gerard is going to fuck you up for this shit."

"Do unto others as you would have them do unto you, and whatever they do unto you, repay them ten folds," replied Belac.

"Who the fuck are you and where in the hell did you hear that?" asked his former colleague as he shook with fear.

"Who I 'am, is the least of your concerns. Now tell me what I want to know and I might call the paramedics. And by the looks of things, all that blood, you could really use a doctor and I'm sure the pain that you're in is excruciating. So decide what you want, a doctor or to bleed out in the street?" exclaimed Belac. Giving him a minute to think things through, Belac patiently waits across the street until his former colleague comes to his senses. Then screaming out in agonizing pain, Belac's former colleague agrees to Belac's terms, if he promised to call an ambulance. After reaching a mutual agreement, by the terms of information in exchange for medical support, Belac's former partner divulges some critical information and gives him an address. Then shouting out loud he said, "Ok it's your turn, call the ambulance."

"A deal is a deal" Belac replied. Taking out his cell phone, Belac dials the emergency operator and waits for an answer.

"What's your emergency?" asked the operator.

"My mistake, I accidentally pressed the wrong speed dial number. My apologies, sorry to waste your time." exclaimed Belac. With a look of betrayal on his face, as Belac ends the call and walks away, Belac's former colleague screamed out, "You fucking bastard, damn you to hell." Without a shred of remorse, Belac continues walking then gets into his vehicle and drives off, leaving his former colleague dressed in black attire to bleed out in the street.

CHAPTER: X

The Motel

After his confrontation with his former colleague, Belac drives to the other side of town to a secluded yet prominent motel. Pulling up to the front entrance, Belac stops at the security booth and shows his room key. Examining his rough appearance, the security officer looks at Belac suspiciously then directs him to the back of the property to Room 112. Displaying his annoyance for being delayed, Belac glares at the security officer then speeds off.

Anxiously awaiting his arrival, Andrea rushes towards the door the moment she hears it open and greets Belac with a smile and a kiss. Noticing that Belac was a little tense, Andrea affectionately asked, "What's the matter, honey?"

"Nothing," replied Belac. After hearing his dispassionate response, Andrea decides to take matters into her own hands and leads Belac romantically. As they strolled into the bedroom, Andrea turns to Belac and kisses him passionately on the lips then pushes him onto the bed. Then behaving erotically, Andrea engages Belac with a seductive slow dance as she unbuttons her blouse. Biting her lips and gently caressing her bountiful breast, Andrea rubs her stomach as she tugs on her underwear then provocatively slides off her skirt. Aroused by Andrea's tantalizing body, Belac decides to dive into temptation and takes off his shirt, revealing his sculpted arms and bulging chest. Enticed and ready for action, Belac signals Andrea over then pulls her on top of him and begins kissing her about the neck. Demonstrating his strength, Belac scoops Andrea up as she giggles with delight and throws her down onto the bed then the duo engaged, not only in a sexual romp but a day of passion.

After spending a whole day and night together, living out their deep animalistic desires. Sitting up in bed, Andrea and Belac reflected on what a great time they had as they both enjoy a glass of red wine. Feeling satisfied and fulfilled, Andrea flicks her hair back then smiles at Belac. With a bewildered look on his face, Belac asked, "What?"

"Nothing, it's just amazing how much you've change," Andrea answered blissfully as she smiles and sips her wine.

"I see," replied Belac.

"That's what I'm talking about, right there! "Your confidence, your carefree attitude and your unapologetic demeanor. Damn you're making me hot!" exclaimed Andrea. Sipping

some wine, Belac looks at Andrea and said, "So that's what turn you on" Then putting her glass down, Andrea leans over and kisses Belac and says, "Caleb, I love you and I always will. The man that you are, I always knew existed, deep inside; you just had all of that strength, passion and confidence locked away. That's why I kissed Eric; that one spark freed the lion out of his cage and into my arms. And now that we're together, I won't let anyone come between us... especially that bitch Sophie." With her own realization that she was getting hot under the collar, Andrea picks up her glass and drinks a mouthful of wine. Noticing the angry look on Belac's face, Andrea catches an attitude and begins to interrogate him. "Did I touch a nerve? Is there something going on between the two of you, because I need to know why you are so concerned about that little harlot? She's been a thorn in our relationship and I will be damned—"

"I need some more wine," Belac exclaimed as he squints his eyes.

"Of course, honey, that's no problem; anything for you," Andrea said as she reaches over to retrieve the bottle of red wine off the nightstand. Without warning, like an expected head-on collision, Belac grabs the bedside lamp off the nightstand and smashes it into Andrea's skull, just as she turns to give him a refill.

CHAPTER: XI

Truth

Awakened unexpectedly early Monday morning, by the constant ringing of his cell phone, Belac struggles to answer his phone as he tries to reaches for it. To his amazement as he answers the phone, Belac is surprised to hear Sophie's voice on the other end of the phone. "Caleb, where are you?" asks Sophie. Still in a daze and trying to catch himself Belac replies, "Sophie, it's 7:30 in the morning, I'm in bed!" In total disbelief Sophie says, "Caleb, did you forget about Phillip? We we're supposed to at the court-house today to post bail for Phillip, remember?

"I forgot. Sorry, that slipped my mind," says Belac.

After apologizing, Belac says, "Ok, here is the plan for today; I'll go straight to the bank and get my half of the bail money and I'll meet you down by the court house in an hour."

"Ok, that sounds like a plan. However, I should inform you that I have already gotten the money. I will get things started here with Phillip and by the time you arrive, we should be ready to go and all you have to do is give me your half when you get here," said Sophie.

"How did you... never mind, I'll see you at the courthouse," replied Belac. Then with a hint of jealousy coursing through her veins, Sophie curiously asked,

"So did you get to meet up with Andrea?"

"Yes, I did but only for a moment. It was a short-lived experience, so I ended things with her," answered Belac.

"I guess you two, didn't really have much in common after all." Sophie said with a smile.

"No we didn't," replied Belac, "I'll see you in an hour."

Later at the courthouse, Sophie patiently waits in line for forty-five minutes, in great anticipation of helping her friend. After her long wait, it was finally her turn to be served as she reaches the front of the line. With the sound of the bell, Sophie quickly approaches the cashier's window and introduces herself then states that she is posting bail for Phillip Kelly.

"One moment Ms. Carter, while I check for his name" replied the cashier. After perusing the list, the cashier looks at her and said, "Mr. Kelly's bail is set for Thirty thousand dollars."

Then going into her purse Sophie pulls out a cashier's check for that amount and hands it to the cashier. The cashier takes the check and inspects it closely and asked, "I'm sorry, what did you say your name was again?" Skeptical about why the cashier would ask for her name, Sophie said, "I told you, my name is Sophitia Carter."

"Do you have any identification, Ms. Carter?" asked the cashier.

"Yes, as a matter of a fact, I do," answered Sophie angrily, as she hands over her driver's license. Taking Sophie's license, the cashier looks at it closely then gives it to a male police officer to photocopy. While returning with Sophie's driver's license, the officer begins flicking the license, then all of a sudden he said, "There's something familiar about this name Carter, I can't put my finger on it but it rings a bell."

Just then as the officer was about to give the cashier back Sophie's driver's license, he notices Phillip's name on the release form and exclaimed, "I know that name, Kelly! Tell me, is he related to Gerard Kelly?"

Sophie answered, "Yes, he is. Gerard Kelly is his father."

With a look of astonishment on his face, the officer stares at Sophie and said, "Yes, I remember now. I can't believe I forgot those famous names, but then again it has been about twenty years."

With a perplexed look on her face, Sophie asked, "What are you talking about?"

"Nothing, just forget that I said anything at all," replied the officer.

Feeling irate about the mystery that surrounds Phillip, his father and herself, Sophie slams her fists onto the counter and shouted, "Tell me, what you are hiding; I want to know the truth."

Rubbing his chin the officer replied, "Ok, I guess you have the right to know." Then the officer asked, "Tell me, are you related to Ian Carter?"

"Yes, he is my father." Sophie answered. Then the officer takes a deep breath and said. "Tell me, Ms. Carter, did you know what kind of business your father was involved in?" shaking her head, Sophie said, "No. All, I could remember is that he used to be gone a lot."

"Sophie, this may come as a surprise to you, but your father, Ian Carter, was a retrieval expert or in other words he was a mob bounty hunter. It was his job to, rough up anyone who didn't pay their loans or gambling debts in the time promised. Your father was very good at what he did. He made quite a name for himself."

Surprised and shocked by what she just heard, Sophie exclaimed, "My dad... a bounty hunter? That's impossible. My father was a kind and gentle man; he wouldn't do the things you said. I don't believe you!"

"Believe it or not, that's what he was. You said you wanted to know the truth, so here it is.! I was assigned to a team focused on bringing your father into custody, but I... we couldn't get him. Through fear alone, your father eluded the justice system for years. No one would talk about or even bring a single charge against him. I wanted to be the one to put him behind bars but he died before that could happen. When rumors, of his death surfaced, I had to find out who killed him, who was brave enough to take on Ian and live to tell the tale. So I began investigating some of his known associates, mainly Gerard Kelly. I guess you're wondering why. You see, Sophie, your father used to work for your friend, Phillip's father. For months, I agonized and inquired about your father's murder, but it was futile. I was desperate for any lead and I wanted badly to know who killed Ian. Then one day an eyewitness came forward, but disappeared after he gave a detailed account of what he saw. The eyewitness reported seeing a white vehicle leaving your father's residence with a little girl; I'm guessing that little girl was you. He said he also saw a black SUV pulling into the driveway as your father walked back inside his house. The witness claims to have heard gunshots fired after the men entered the home, so he hid himself."

Heartbroken and grieved by the details of her father's death, tears begin to stream down Sophie's face as she starts to weep. Then Sophie cries out, "Stop it, stop your lies."

"Officer Reilly, that's enough. Can't you see the poor girl is in shambles?" exclaimed the cashier as she stamps the forms for Phillip's release.

Then Officer Reilly exclaimed, "She wanted to know truth; now she does. But there's more. The witness also reported seeing another sedan, parked out front. While spying, the eyewitness reported seeing another gentleman wearing a stylish suit enter your home. The witness said he heard another gunshot fired, then he saw the same gentleman exit your father's house and drove off. The witness identified that gentleman as Gerard Kelly. So the truth is Gerard Kelly, Phillip Kelly's father, killed your father, Ian Carter."

CHAPTER: XII

You're Father, My Father

"So now you know the truth about your father, how he lived and died," said Officer Reilly. As reality sets in, Sophie stands there petrified by the traumatizing truth of her father's life and death. With tears built up in her eyes, Sophie squeezes the forms in her hand then flees towards the exit, sobbing bitterly. Desperately trying to escape the heartbreaking truth about her father, Sophie pushes her way through the door and crashes into Belac.

"Whoa, slow down," exclaimed Belac.

"Sorry, I...I have to go," Sophie replied as tears rolled down her face.

Then noticing that Sophie was distraught, Belac takes hold of her hand and asked, "Sophie, what's the matter, why are you crying?" Trying to pull away, Sophie yells, "Caleb, let me go! Just leave me alone. Let me go!"

"Sophie, what's wrong? Are they not releasing Phillip?" Belac asked as he struggles against Sophie in a tug of war. After succumbing to the post-traumatic stress about the truth of her father, Sophie breaks down and drops to the floor weeping. "They killed him!" With great concern Belac grabs Sophie and consoles her then asked, "What happened to Phillip, who killed him?"

"Phillip is fine, but my father, they killed him," Sophie replied faintly as she phased out of reality. With a confused look on his face Belac exclaimed, "Who killed your father?" Unresponsive with tears flowing down her face, Belac tries to snap Sophie out of her current state of shock, but it was of no use as Sophie remained zoned out. Realizing that something traumatic had to have occurred prior to his arrival, Belac decides to investigate and find out what happened. After his investigation, Belac carries Sophie to the car and straps her into the front passenger seat.

About thirty minutes later, after achieving the goal they had set out to complete, Belac desperately tries again to wake Sophie out of her catatonic state but once again, his efforts were futile. Then all of a sudden, Sophie does something strange and out of character: she begins unbuttoning her blouse, revealing a necklace that she took hold of and clinched very tightly.

"When I was five years old, my father gave me this necklace; it belonged to my mother and it's the only thing of hers that I have. I never knew my mother, only of her sacrifice dying after giving birth to me and of her love of Japanese jewelry and art. I was given this pendant, to always have something to remember her by." Sophie sniffled as she spoke.

Holding the pinkish-red pendant in her hand, Sophie kisses it lovingly as she slowly pressed it against her lips then exclaimed. "I've always known about my mother and how she gave her life to save mine, and for that I will forever be indebted to her." After lamenting about her mother, Sophie looks outside the window then releases the pendant and said, "When my father died, my grandmother told me he went to a better place; she never told me how he died or what kind of person he was... no one did, until today. Now I know the truth about my father and what kind of man he truly was."

With her heart broken and heavy, Sophie pauses for a moment and wipes her tears as she sniffles. Then revealing the truth about her father, Sophie said, "Now thinking about it, it's amazing how my father could have live that kind of life and still showed me so much loved. As a child, I knew my dad loved me a lot. I can still recall when he took me for ice cream, how he used to take me for walks in the park and how he used to push me on the swing. That's the kind of man my father was and that's how I remember him. But now, to be told that my father had another life, a life I knew nothing about, a life as a mob debt collector and was killed by...."

"Sophie!" Belac shouted.

"Don't interrupt me, let me finish," replied Sophie.

"I told myself it was a lie, but deep inside I knew it was the truth. Why else would Officer Reilly feel so compelled to tell me about our fathers and how they lived, just after recognizing both our last names? Now I know things about my father, I wish I didn't, like the name of his murder. Officer Reilly not only told me about my father's life, but he revealed key details about his death and of a witness who was at the scene. He said the witness reported seeing a child, me, leaving with my grandmother in a white sedan. He also reported seeing some men, enter my father's house and shortly afterwards hearing multiple gunshots fired. What the witness said next was the most shocking. He said everything went quiet for a moment, then he heard one final gunshot fired and reported seeing a man walking outside. The witness described and identified that man as Gerard Kelly."

"What!" shouted Phillip.

"I'll break it down for you: Phillip. Your father killed my father!" exclaimed Sophie.

CHAPTER: XIII

Flashback

With the revelation of Sophie's father murderer being Gerard Kelly, Phillip's father, a dispute breaks out between Phillip and Sophie as they get into a quarrel.

"Sophie, are you serious, you actually think my father killed your father?" shouted Phillip.

"Yes, of course I do," replied Sophie.

"You're delusional. Sophie listen to yourself, you're suggesting that my father, murdered your father," exclaimed Phillip. As if things couldn't get any worse, Sophie loosens her seatbelt, turns back to Phillip and shouted, "I'm not suggesting, that's what I just said. Your murderous father killed my…"

"Alright, that's enough. Both of you calm down!" Belac exclaimed as he slammed the car brakes. Then pausing for a moment, he said, "This is a lot to deal with right now; let's all take a break and cool off for a minute and we'll continue this discussion later."

"Ok, fine. Then maybe we can get some clarification," answered Phillip.

"Clarification! I doubt it," answered Sophie.

With a stern look on his face, Belac looks at Phillip and Sophie then continued driving as they settle down. Two minutes later, after driving in complete silence, Belac proclaimed, "Phillip, first thing we have to do is get you a fresh change of clothes then we'll head to the office. Afterwards, Phillip, you, Sophie and I, will get together and figure all this stuff out. So until then, not a word to anyone, understood?" Belac exclaimed as he looked at Sophie. In agreeance with what Belac said, Phillip replies, "Understood." Sophie nods her head and sighs, "Ok."

Then all of a sudden as all appeared to be going well as they drove in silence, Phillip shouted, "What I don't understand is how you, Sophie, could believe the words of a total stranger you just met. Granted he's an officer of the law, but this Officer Reilly sounded like he had a personal vendetta against my dad, so why should I believe anything he had to say? I admit my dad is not a saint but to come up with a story that your father, beat up dead beats for my dad?! Is ludicrous! Now all of a sudden, after all this time, a witness says he heard gun shots fired and claims to have seen my dad leave your father's house after supposingly murdering your father is preposterous. My dad's a mob boss who kills his employees, is laughable. I just want to know why, it's so easy for you to believe that my dad killed your dad, flared Phillip. After voicing his vexation with Sophie's allegation against his father, Belac tries to calm Phillip down, but fails in his attempt to do so, as Sophie cut's him off and defends the claim that his father killed her father.

"I believe him because I remember it, like it was just yesterday. The last time, I saw him." Sophie sighed.

At that moment, a look of sadness comes on Sophie's face as tears begin to well up in her eyes and memories of that day begin to surface as she reminisces on her final memory with her father.

"Mirror, mirror on the wall who is the most beautifulest of them all?" said Eight -year- old Sophie.

"You are Kichona," said her father in a deep comforting voice as he rubbed her shoulder gently.

"Really, Daddy?" asked eight-year old Sophie, as she blushed looking up at her father.

"Of course, honey! Any prince would be lucky to have you as his queen," exclaimed her father. After displaying some fatherly love towards his daughter, he smiles and puts a coat on her, then says, "Sweetheart, beautifulest is not a real word."

"Why isn't it a real word if, you can say it?" asked Sophie. Just then as Sophie's father was about to explain; why beautifulest is not a real word, a car horn honks and interrupts the tender father-daughter moment. "That's your grandmother, we better get going," said her father. Taking her by the hand, Sophie's father walks her to the car and hugged her affectionately and says, "Sophie, you, be a good girl for your grandmother, ok?"

"Yes, Daddy, I promise," exclaimed Sophie as she hugs her father tightly. Then she says, "Bye, bye Daddy. I love you," as she enters the vehicle and her dad closes the car door behind her.

"I love you too! Kichona," her father said with a smile. Just then the driver's window rolls down and Sophie's grandmother says, "Ian, you have to stop this. When will you give up this life you are living? Sophie is getting bigger and she is going to need her father to be there for her and protect her. Not to endanger her life. You are going to have to make a decision."

"I already have; after this I'm out. Evelyn everything is going to be fine, you'll see," replied Ian.

In disbelief of what Ian said to her, Evelyn rolls up the window and leaves.

... Then I saw the black SUV pull into my driveway.

CHAPTER: XIV

Death Notice

Meanwhile at Global Media, Mr. Blackwell is about to conduct a manager's meeting; however, Caleb is not present and Eric is up to his despicable ways, once again.

"Mr. Blackwell, with all due respect, sir, we have to start this meeting. We can't hold everyone hostage, just because one inconsiderate individual chooses not to show up. What kind of example are we setting?" asked Eric wickedly. Contemplating about what Eric said, Mr. Blackwell gives the signal for everyone to settle down as the meeting begins. "Don't worry, Mr. Blackwell; I will personally deal with Caleb for his total disrespect towards you and for not attending this meeting" whispered Eric menacingly. Ten minutes into the meeting, the mandatory manager's meeting comes to an alarming halt as the doors of the executive office fly wide open and Detectives Granger and Storr come bursting through.

"What the hell do you think you're doing? This is a private meeting; you have no right to come barging in here like this!" shouted Eric.

"Shut up you pompous jackass," sneered Detective Storr.

"Were here on official police business. We have some questions and we'd like for them to be answered," said Detective Granger. Outraged by the Detective's intrusion, Mr. Blackwell stands to his feet and exclaimed, "What is the meaning of this!"

"Police business. I thought we made that clear already," replied Detective Storr. After a few seconds of pacing back and forth, Detective Granger looks around the room and asked "Does the name Andrea O'Brien, ring a bell?"

"Of course it does, she's the Sales and Marketing, office supervisor," replied Mr. Blackwell.

"Well she was," exclaimed Detective Storr.

With a look of concern, Eric asked, "What are you saying, Detective?"

"Ms. O'Brien was found dead in a motel room," exclaimed Detective Granger. Devastated by the news of Andrea's death, Mr. Blackwell flops down into his chair and exclaimed, "Not again."

"This can't be; are you sure it was Andrea you found?" asked Eric.

"Yeah, and she was dolled up real nice too, what a pity," said Detective Storr.

"Please excuse, Detective Storr. Andrea was with someone and they had red wine and enjoyed other pleasures," explained Detective Granger.

"How did she die?" asked Mr. Blackwell.

"Blunt force trauma to the head. Andrea was struck on the head with a bedside lamp and was left there to bleed to death," answered Detective Granger.

"Does anyone in this room, know who Andrea might have been planning to meet up with; or know of anyone she may have had an issue with on the job? Or maybe knows of anyone who just didn't like her at all?" asked Detective Storr.

Immediately following Detective Storr's pertinent questions, Belac, Sophie and Phillip come charging through the doors arguing and causing a ruckus.

"There they are detectives," said Eric as he pointed them out.

With all eyes on them and stares from everywhere, confusion comes on their faces as they looked around. Then Phillip looks at Sophie, Sophie looks at Belac and Belac looks at them and then they all look at Eric.

"Detective, I present to you, the answers to your questions: the boyfriend, the mistress and the insubordinate," Eric smiled sadistically. In response to Eric's accusation, Belac clinched his fist and said, "Eric! Whatever the hell this is, you will pay."

"Enough!" retorted Detective Granger.

"Actually, Bryan, I was going to let that one play out," Detective Storr exclaimed sarcastically.

"Hey hotshot, your girlfriend Andrea, was found dead." exclaimed Detective Granger.

In a sequence of events in relation to hearing the startling announcement of Andrea's death, Sophie puts her hand over her mouth and sighed "Oh my God." With a genuine look of compassion on his face Phillip exclaimed, "What!" Then very smugly, Belac asked, "So you think one of us did it?"

Then Detective Granger said, "Caleb, we're detectives and it's our job to investigate all possible leads until we discover the truth or the best acceptable reason for the course of action or actions taken, that lead to the unfavorable outcome such as this one."

"Does that answer your question?" asked Detective Storr.

"More or less," replied Belac.

"Mr. Blackwell, with your permission we'd like to use one of your offices for questioning," asked Detective Granger.

"You can use my office; it's right over there," declared Eric freely. After entering Eric's office, both Detectives Granger and Storr confront the three-o in an effort to narrow down a suspect and find a motive. "Caleb, let's cut to the chase; your girlfriend was found dead in a compromising position, if you know what I mean," stated Detective Storr.

"According to the security officer on duty, a man, fitting your description came to see Andrea and spent the night and left the next day. In conjunction with the autopsy, we know she died Sunday. Can you give an account of your whereabouts?" Detective Granger sneered as he poked.

"Yes, I can. Andrea and I spent the day together but I assure you, she was alive and kicking. If you know what I mean," replied Belac.

"So you both spent the entire day in a motel?" asked Detective Granger.

Just then Sophie unintentionally blurts out, "She was found in a motel!" With the spotlight on her, Sophie goes quiet as she remembers what Belac had said to her earlier that morning, when she asked him about meeting up with Andrea. "Yes, I did but only for a moment. It was a short lived experience, so I ended things with her."

"You just remembered something, didn't you" shouted Detective Storr.

"No," Sophie answered nervously.

"Yes you did. That look on your face, says it all. So spill it," demanded Detective Granger. Suddenly a call comes through on Detective Granger's cell phone and he reluctantly, answers it. Thirty seconds later Detective Granger hangs up the phone and said "We got a hit on the prints"

"Yeah, who?" asked Detective Storr

"You won't believe it... Ian Carter," answered Detective Granger.

CHAPTER: XV

Unanswered Question

"So a dead man's fingerprints shows up again," scoffed Detective Storr.

"I'm still trying to figure out, how does, Ian Carter fingerprints keep finding their way, in yet another murder investigation?" asked Detective Granger. Struggling with the sorrow of hearing her father's name being mentioned, a tear falls free from Sophie's eye as she looks furiously at Phillip. Then in a brittle voice Sophie cries out "Why won't your father, let my father rest in peace!"

"Sophie, my father didn't kill your father!" exclaimed Phillip. Then all of a sudden, Sophie starts screaming and yelling "Yes he did, you're father killed my father. Your daddy is a murderer!" Then Phillip shouted "Sophie for the last time, my father didn't kill your dad! How the hell, you could go around accusing my Father of murder and you don't even know what happen"

"That's enough! Both of you calm down" said Belac sternly. Then as things settled down, Belac looks at both Detectives and asked "aren't you guys going to say anything?"

"Nope!" answered both Detectives, simultaneously as they looked at each other.

"You see young fella, this is what we do" answered Detective Storr,

"When a little pressure is applied, people start talking and you just never know what they may say" Detective Granger explained as he prepares to leave, then he said "You, folks have been quite helpful. Mr. Kelly we'll be in touch"

After fixing his coat, Detective Storr turns to Sophie and said "Ms. Carter it's been a pleasure" then both Detectives depart.

After the Detective's departure, things begin to cycle out of control as Sophie exhibits her anger towards Phillip and leers at him with disgust then storms out the office. Trying to stop her, Belac exclaimed "Sophie wait" but it was too late as Sophie ignores Belac and exits through the door. Following Sophie's departure, Phillip decides to go his way and pushes pass Belac, making his way towards the exit. "Hey, where are you going?" asked Belac.

"I'm going to see my father, he's the only one that can clear up this mess and besides I have questions that need answering," replied Phillip.

Nodding his head Belac throws Phillip his key and said, "Alright, do what you have to do, we'll catch up later. Right now, I have to handle things with Sophie". In agreeance with Belac, Phillip exclaimed "Ok" then he leaves.

Succeeding the calamity of the three-o's tragic split, Belac excuses himself from the meeting, to track down Sophie. Checking behind every door, Belac relentless search takes him to the staff break room, where he finds Sophie in the corner crying. Gently calling out to Sophie, Belac walks over and tries to comfort for her. With tears continuously falling from her cheek, Sophie slowly turns to Belac and embraces him tightly while sobbing bitterly. "Caleb, why did they have to kill my father … why?" sniffled, Sophie.

"I don't know," replied Belac then he said "Let's get out of here; I know a place where we can go and talk." Wiping her tears and sniffling, Sophie agrees to an evening get together then asked, "You think I'll ever find out, what really happen?"

Meanwhile on the other side of town, fueled with rage of its driver, screeched the midnight blue Impala as it hurdles fiercely towards the front entrance of Legacy Auto, mega car-lot. Alarmed by the impending vehicle approaching the premises, the security team prepares for a confrontation but instead of a showdown, the sedan slides in front of the gate. Immediately as the vehicle comes to a complete stop, the entire security detail run towards the offending automobile and surrounds the vehicle, military style. Prepared for an altercation, the security team earnestly waits for the daredevil driving the out of control automobile to reveal him or herself. Then the car door swings open and the team gets their wish as Phillip exits the vehicle in a hostile manner with one goal in mind. With the revelation that the driver of the Impala was Phillip, the head security officer gives the order to stand down.

"It's Mr. Kelly's son, stand down" he commanded. Without remorse for the commotion he caused, Phillip boldly walks inside his father's business establishment like a bulldozer on a mission. "You can't, come barging in here, like you own the place. You need an appointment, just like everyone else, if you want to see Mr. Kelly!" shouted Gerard's secretary. Paying no attention to her, Phillip smirked and said, "Watch me" then continuing on his mission, Phillip pushes open his father's door and asked the daunting question "Did you kill Ian carter?"

CHAPTER XVI

Confrontation

"**N**ow then, that's my boy! So they finally drop and a man emerges. It seems like you're finally ready to take over the family business," smirked Gerard.

"Dad I don't have time for this, when will you understand that I don't want anything to do with your business, I'm happy with my life and who I 'am," exclaimed Phillip.

"Hmph, how you disappoint me, again and again. Phillip, when I was your age I had a dream... a dream of building an empire and of course I achieved that goal. Then I had another dream and in this dream I had a son, who would take over the family business and expand it. Then one day, he would pass it on to his son and his son to his son and so on, but that dream has turned into a fucking nightmare! Oh Yeah, now I have a son, a son who has no fucking ambition! And who wants to see everything I worked so hard for go down the fucking toilette," shouted Gerard.

"I'm sorry, am not the son you wanted or dreamed about dad! But I have my own life and I have a right to live it the way I want and I choose not to live it in your footsteps, now answer the gad damn question! Did you or did you not killed Ian Carter?" asked Phillip.

"I did," Gerard, answered openly.

Stunned by his father's callous answer and carefree attitude, a look of astonishment comes across Phillip's face then he asked his father "How could you be so cold and emotionless like that?"

"It's simple; I merely did what had to be done, Ian was a cancer that needed to be cut out and so, I did... But why the sudden interest in Ian Carter?" asked Gerard.

"Not that you care... but Ian, left behind a daughter, her name is Sophie and she is a friend and she just learnt the name of her father's killer. Now imagine my surprise, when that friend confronts me and accuses my father of being of her father's murder" replied Phillip. Reclining back in his chair, Gerard bites his lower lip and said "Wow that must have been an uncomfortable conversation. I will have to send her some flowers for her lost."

"You are unbelievable. I don't know even know why I wasted my time coming here. I'm out of here," shouted Phillip.

"Phillip wait, don't you want to know why?" Gerard asked provokingly.

Aggravated by his father's cold-hearted admission to murdering Ian, Phillip turns back and answered "Why! What?"

"Why the reason, I killed Ian, off course," replied Gerard

"Alright dad, I'll bite. Why did you kill Ian?" asked Phillip. Then getting up from his chair, Gerard walks over to his cabinet and takes out two rock glasses and a bottle of Jack Daniels then pours a drink for Phillip and one for himself. Afterwards, he walks back over to Phillip and hands him the glass then invites Phillip to have a seat. After taking a sip of his alcoholic beverage, Gerard reveals to his son, why he killed Ian.

"I know you think the worst about me and many others share your exact sentiments too but coming up back in the day wasn't easy. Phillip, I was a hustler. I ate, whatever I could find, I did what I had to, just to survive and I did. About **20years** ago, I started living my dream and all that I had envisioned for myself and everything I wanted finally, started to manifest. I had money, women, cars, I was envied but most of all, I had respect! My rivals feared me and partly because I had Ian on my side. Ian was a bad ass; he had no fear, this guy use to break bones just for fun. No matter the target, he always got the job done and with style and I, Gerard Kelly had his loyalty. Then one day out of the blue, he comes to me and says "He's out", he wanted out the game. Son surely even you know, I couldn't let him walk away just like that; I had an image to maintain and allowing him to walk away would made me appear weak and everything I had fought for up to that point would of being in vein. I knew, if I wanted to keep my position at the top, I would of had to been the one, to take him out. So I came up with a plan and agreed to his request, under one condition that he complete one, final job for me. He agreed to do so but he didn't know that was going to be his last job ever. The crew got together and went to retrieve the asset as planned but to Ian's surprise, he was the one to be put him down, the boys knew how far to go and not to kill him, that pleasure was to be savored by me only. So when I got the call that he was down, I walked inside, took out my berretta and pulled the trigger. Hmph... before Ian died; he chanted some kind of prayer. He was the spiritual type and he always believed if he died, he would be recanted as someone else." said Gerard.

"So that's why you killed him, because he wanted out?" asked Phillip

"Yes, that's the reason, why I killed Ian," answered Gerard.

CHAPTER XVII

Date Night

Later that evening, casually dining at an Italian bistro, Belac and Sophie are enjoying a tasty meal. "Mmm, the food here is so amazing and the garlic bread is to die for. Caleb, how did you ever find this place, it's so... not you," exclaimed Sophie.

"I'm glad you like it," replied Belac.

"I like it a lot," Sophie responded with a smile as she stared deeply into his eyes.

"It's good to see a smile back on your face," said Belac.

"Thanks to you," blushed Sophie. While staring into each other eyes, Belac puts his hand on top of Sophie's and gently caresses it. As the evening progressed, Belac and Sophie, inadvertently enjoys a tender evening, until a clumsy waitress bumps into their table and knock overs there drinks. "Oh! I'm terribly sorry, I tripped… did I spill any drink on you?" asked the waitress apologetically.

"No you didn't but our drinks, however," replied Sophie.

"Yes of course, what can I get you?" asked the Waitress

"I'll have a glass of white wine," replied Sophie.

"And sir, what will you be having?" the Waitress asked earnestly.

"I'll have a club soda with lime and ice," answered Belac.

"If that is all, I'll be back shortly with your beverages," exclaimed the Waitress. As the Waitress hurried of, to complete the drink orders, Sophie decides to have some fun and tease Belac. "A club soda with lime?" Sophie asked factiously.

"Yes I don't drink alcoholic beverage before **6pm,**" answered Belac.

"So what, you have a Dr. Jekyll and Mr. Hyde thing going," laughed Sophie. Then after an exchange of playful banter, Sophie looks at the time on her watch and said "Hey! Its **5:53 pm,** surly Caleb you could have a drink."

"Okay, I concede," laughed Belac.

"Great! But you can't order, until I get back. I have to powder my nose," exclaimed Sophie.

Fifteen minutes later, taking her seat, Sophie returns to the table and said, "Sorry for the wait but there was a line." Then looking around and behaving strangely, Belac looks at Sophie and blurted, "Kichona!" With her eyes widen and jaw dropped, Sophie stares at Belac as she is shocked to be called Kichona and said, "Caleb, you called me Kichona. My father's gave me that nickname, when I was a child, it must be a sign." Then smiling to herself, she asked "Did you know? Kichona is Japanese for precious." In the midst of Sophie's explanation on how her father gave her the childhood nick- name Kichona, the waitress returns to the table and apologies for the long wait. Giving Sophie her glass of wine, the waitress turns to Belac and hands him, his beverage. Upon receiving his club soda, Belac becomes increasingly angry and then the confusion begins. "What is this?" asked Belac.

"That's the club soda with lime and Ice that you ordered," replied the waitress.

"Yeah Kay, that's the drink you ordered honey," Sophie answered with a smile.

"Don't call me that," exclaimed Belac.

"Ok, calm down, what's the matter with you?" asked Sophie.

"Take this away and get me a real drink," snarled Belac

"Ok sir, no problem. What can I get you?" the waitress asked politely.

"I want a Manhattan cocktail!" exclaimed Belac.

"Yes, right away sir" the waitress replied respectfully. After the waitress leaves, Sophie exclaimed, "Caleb that was rude! What is the matter with you? It's like you changed into someone else all of a sudden". Then in an attempt to connect with Belac, Sophie reaches for his hand and tries to place her hand on top his but Belac instantly retracts his hand and asked, "What are you doing?

"I thought you like the touching my hand," Sophie said with a smile as she tried to grab his other hand. But her plans were foiled, as Belac perceives her goal and quickly removes his hand before she could take hold of it. While withdrawing his hand, Sophie notices a strange tattoo on Belac's wrist as his shirtsleeve slides up and reveals a mysterious marking on his skin. "I've never noticed that tattoo before, when did you get that?" asked Sophie.

Pilling down his shirtsleeve to conceal the tattoo, Belac opens his mouth to answer Sophie, when all of a sudden the waitress returns and informs Belac that she was unable to complete his drink order.

"I'm sorry, sir, but we are out of Angostura bitters; is there another drink that you would like?" asked the waitress.

"No!" Belac shouted.

Then as the waitress tries to apologize, Belac stands up and shouted, "Don't bother." Then taking out a $100-dollar bill, Belac slams it onto the table and storms out of the restaurant angrily. Baffled by Belac's sudden switch in personality, Sophie and the waitress look at each other, then the waitress asked, "What just happened?" Unable to process the unusual flow of events, Sophie shrugs her shoulders and said, "I'm not sure and at this point, I don't even know who he is."

CHAPTER: XVIII

The Last Piece

After abruptly leaving the restaurant, Belac becomes increasingly disoriented as images of a little girl playing princess begin to bombard his mind, following his encounter with Sophie. Distraught and unaware of where he was aimlessly walking, Belac finds himself a few blocks away from the restaurant as he struggles to clear his mind. Fighting to keep his composure, Belac stops in an alley to gather his thoughts as he is challenged by an apparent nervous breakdown. With the effects of a mental disorder, attempting to claim his sanity, Belac somehow digs deep within and finds the will power to overcome the sudden paranoia. Now with his head back in the game, Belac checks his surroundings and notices a sign across the street on a building that reads "Respect." Upon continual surveillance of the area, Belac notices a scrappy looking male performing an unusual knock on the door of that particular building and instantly remembers what his former colleague, from the accident, had told him. Then looking around, Belac suddenly realizes that he was right where he needed to be. Inspired with the hope of being one-step closer to achieving his goal, Belac focuses on the eminent task ahead, as he is fueled with a renewed determination. Hurrying across the street in an attempt to gain access to the same building, Belac mimics the same unusual knock that he saw earlier and a doorman answers the door.

"What's the password?" the doorman asked as he opens the peephole.

Recalling what his former colleague had told him, Belac recites the password and gains access inside. Entering the secret hall, Belac looks around and thinks to himself, *"Everything is exactly as was told,"* pool tables, card games and sports betting all being played as he walked through the hall. After scoping out the underground hall, Belac walks over to the bar and takes a seat as he waits to be served. Then casually walking to him, the bartender decides to come over and serve, Belac. While coming over, the bartender analyzes Belac, as she watches him suspiciously and asked, "What will it be?" Ordering his famous drink Belac replied, "I'll have a Manhattan cocktail with an olive." Pausing for a moment the bartender said "That's an, O.G. drink. What are you doing in a place like this?"

"What's it to you?" asked Belac.

"I've never seen you in here before and this don't look like your kind of place, so what are you really doing in here?" the bartender asked as she gives Belac, his drink. Taking a sip, Belac takes out a thousand dollars and holds it up and responded, "Looks can be deceiving; I'm here for the big game, the one played in the back." Giving him the ok, the bartender buzzes the door and directs Belac to the back. Finishing his drink, Belac makes a beeline to the high stakes room in the back. Upon entering the high stakes room, Belac is confronted with a revolver pointed at his head. To Belac's surprise the person across the room that was giving the order for a second henchman to search him, was another familiar face that he knew all too well.

"He's clean, boss," said the second henchman.

After his apparent pat down, the man in charge instructs Maurice, his henchman to let him through and invites Belac to have a seat. With a hostile look on his face, as Belac walks over to take a seat, Maurice mean mugs Belac then puts his gun back in its holster on his chest.

"Tell me, what can I do for you?" asked his former friend in charge.

"I'm here for the big game; I believe its five grand to play," Belac answered, as he stared into his former colleague's eyes.

"I don't believe we've met before. How did you come to know about our operation?" asked Belac's former colleague.

"An old acquaintance told me about this place. He said if I was interested, I could make some big money. So here I 'am," answered Belac.

All of a sudden, the dastardly trio begins laughing and making fun of Belac, showing their total lack of respect for him. Annoyed by their folly, Belac takes out an envelope and throws five thousand dollars on the table. The laughter stops as Belac's former companion picks up the five grand and exclaimed, "You're serious." Then looking at Belac intently, he said, "My friend, look around, does it look like we play poker in here? Now I don't know where you got that information, but you were misinformed; now while I'm still in a good mood, get the fuck up out of here and don't let me see your mug around here again," exclaimed Belac's former companion.

Agreeing to leave based on his former companion's suggestion, Belac opens his hand and requested for his money back, but his former colleague had other plans.

"Your donation will be put to good use; Maurice, escort this gentleman out," said Belac's former colleague. Tapping him on the shoulder, Maurice points Belac to the exit. Rising up from his chair and closely followed by Maurice, Belac is escorted to the door, to ensure that he leaves. As he extends his hand to open the door, Belac spins around and punches Maurice in his face, grabs his gun from his holster and pushes him to the ground. Setting his sights on the other henchman, Belac points the revolver and shoots him twice in the chest. Then firing a warning shot at his former companion just before he has time to draw his weapon, Belac shakes his head as if to say, "Don't even think about it." Still aware of Maurice's presence, Belac looks back and shoots him in the stomach. Then in a desperate attempt to save his own life, Belac's former companion begins to bargain as he offers Belac a deal; the return of his five grand with fifty percent interest in exchange for his life. But Belac denies his offer and shoves the revolver in his face and interrogates him.

"I don't give a damn about the money. Just tell me where I can find Gerard," Belac demanded sternly.

"Forget it, I'm not telling you shit!" exclaimed his former colleague.

After his former colleague refuses to talk, Belac's patience wears thin as he gets angry and shoots his former companion twice in his right leg. Then very savagely, Belac drives his foot into his former colleague's wounded leg and pistol whips him, until he disclosed everything he wanted to know. Suddenly to Belac's amazement the office door is kicked wide open, as the bartender comes bursting through firing a deadly shot at him, with a 12 gauge shotgun. Quickly jumping out of harm's way, Belac lands near the other henchman and scampers over to his lifeless body and acquires his handgun. Dashing to safety as the bartender readies her weapon, Belac jumps out the way just barely avoiding, becoming a casualty as another relentless shot is fired in his direction. Before slamming into the floor, Belac fires multiple shots at the bartender, resulting in her being shot in the neck and in the chest. After crash landing, Belac struggles to his feet and limps over to the bartender and finishes her off, with a final shot to the head.

CHAPTER: XIX

Revelation

The next day, plagued with the effects of last night's escapade, Belac sits in his office, groggy and aching as he tries to figure out, why he feels the way he does. Unbeknownst to him, Phillip stops by, for an unexpected visit, but after observing Belac's zoned-out appearance, Phillip refrains from the idea of friendly banter and instead decides to engage him in a one on one conversation out of concern for his wellbeing. "Are you ok?" asked Phillip. Still feeling dreary from the night before, Belac looks up and faintly exclaimed, "Hey."

In response to Belac's weary salutation, Phillip said, "You must have had some night."

"If, I did, I can't remember," replied Belac.

"Wow! You really have changed, haven't you, Caleb. Anyway, I came up here looking for Sophie but I was told, she called in today. I was hoping to have a word with her. Turns out my dad did kill her father!" said Phillip.

"Whoa! I know I need to talk to her but that right there is heavy," replied Belac.

"Tell me about it; I don't even know what to say to her. So what's going on with you two?" asked Phillip.

"Well… we went by Antonio's last night and we had a great time, but I can't remember anything after dinner. Everything after that point is just a blur," said Belac. Suddenly, Eric pokes his head in and shouted, "Caleb, meeting in five minutes; hurry up and get your ass in gear!" With the fierceness of an out of control fire, Belac retorted, "Who the hell do you think you're talking to?"

"I don't think, I know who I'm talking to," Eric replied as he walks into Belac's office boldly and uninvited. "If, I tell you to move, then you move; if, I say jump, you ask how high. Do I make myself clear?"

Enraged by Eric's blatant disrespect, Belac jumps to his feet and stands face to face with Eric and said, "Maybe I wasn't clear. I don't know who you think you're talking to, but you obviously got me confused with one of your cronies. But understand this, if you don't get out my office, I'll move your ass." In a moment's notice before the situation could worsen, Phillip quickly parts the two and prevents an altercation from occurring.

"Caleb, Eric! Come on guys, control yourselves. Caleb, calm down he's not worth it. Eric, set an example; you're an assistant director for god's sake! Act with some integrity," exclaimed Phillip. With fire still in their eyes, Eric and Belac continue to stare each other down. Then coming to their senses, Eric and Belac suppressed their dislike for each other and disperse to their meeting.

Meanwhile, on the other side of town, Sophie takes a bus ride and gets off at a theologian information center, to research renowned religions and their practices. Off the bus, up the stairs and through the doors, Sophie walked anxiously into the theologian headquarters. Step by step, Sophie walks cautiously through the empty, poorly lit halls taken by all the bizarre sights. "Hello! Is anyone here?" Sophie asked fearfully, but there was no reply. With no one in sight, Sophie decides to take a look around on her own. While snooping, Sophie's mind begins to play tricks on her as she looks at all the religious relics around her. While viewing the random selections of crosses, symbols and face-masks, Sophie thinks to herself, "This place is really creepy and way too quiet; I need to find what I'm looking for and get the hell out of here fast." Searching diligently through the different sections, skimming through various books, an eerie feeling comes over Sophie as she walks through the aisles. Finally coming across a book that seemed to be just what she was looking for; Sophie fully devotes all of her attention to the pages of that book. With her head deep, down into the book and eyes glued to the pages, Sophie clutches onto every word in each sentence, like a magnet joined to steel, hoping to find the answers that she was looking for. As Sophie continues to read, she comes to the unfortunate realization that the information that she thought she had found, actually wasn't the info that she was so desperately searching for. With her curiosity, piqued, Sophie closes the book, feeling defeated as if all her efforts were in vain. Then taken by surprise, Sophie nearly jumps out of her skin as a mysterious elderly man appears in front of her.

"What is it, you seek?" the curator asked in a deep dreary voice.

Frightened by his ghastly appearance, Sophie stands motionless as her eyes catch sight of the six foot four mysterious curator dressed in black. Freaked out by his frosty colored dreadlocks, impaired eye and grim disposition, Sophie takes one look at the hunched over curator and his archaic staff and decides it's time to leave. With her hands stretched out in front of her, Sophie steps back slowly and exclaimed, "Sorry, I didn't mean to trespass; I'll leave right away." Walking in tandem with her, the curator advances towards Sophie as he asked the same frightful question. "What is it, you seek?" Terrified and filled with fear, Sophie makes a quick 180 degree turn and attempts to run away, but in her haste to escape, Sophie trips over a small statue and hits her head against the floor. Moments later after bumping her head, Sophie awakens dazed and unaware of where she was momentarily, until she heard his voice, "You hit your head pretty hard."

Setting her eyes on the nightmarish curator, Sophie begins screaming uncontrollably. Burdened with the titanic size task of trying to calm Sophie down, the curator exclaimed, "Please don't be frightened, I mean you no harm. Now tell me, what is it you seek?" Taking a deep breath, Sophie said, "I know this might sound crazy, but I was looking for information on my father."

"Can you be more specific? This is a place of divinity," replied the curator.

"Sorry, I mean my biological father," declared Sophie.

"Ok," the curator exclaimed as he raised his eyebrow.

"Twenty years ago my father was murdered in cold blood; I was a little girl when it happened. There are a lot of things I don't recall about my father, but I do remember him having a peculiar tattoo on his back. I can't tell you, what the symbol was or what it meant; I just know it's connected to something religious. Now here's the part that concerns me the most. I have a friend, his name is Caleb and I have known him for quite some time and we work together. The other night we went out for something to eat and everything was going well, we ate, we laughed and we shared a moment, it was magical. Dinner with Caleb was perfect, until I saw a tattoo on the back of his hand as his shirtsleeve slides up. This is where things get interesting because the same tattoo that was on Caleb's hand, is the same tattoo that was on my father's back. I have known Caleb for a couple of years, and he has never had or even mentioned getting a tattoo," explained Sophie.

"Hmmm. That's quite interesting; is there anything else you can tell me?" asked the curator.

"Yes, actually," said Sophie. "He has been acting, strange lately, like he was someone else."

"Oh? How so?" inquired the curator.

"Like I mentioned before, we went out for dinner and we were having a great time then things got weird. His behavior changed and out of the blue he called me "Kichona" Kichona is Japanese for precious. That nick-name was given to me, by my father on my fifth birthday and only he, called me that," exclaimed Sophie.

Intrigued by Sophie's story about her father and friend, the curator walks over to a shelf and grabs a book, then presents it to Sophie and asked, "Is this, the symbol you are referring to?"

With a surprised look on her face, Sophie marvels at the symbol and replied, "Yes, this is the symbol; this is definitely it."

"I thought as much," exclaimed the curator. "This symbol is very unique and is connected to those who believe in the rebirth of reincarnation, also known as (re-pneuma). This religion is based on the belief of transmigration of the spirit. Transferal of the spirit can best be described as jumping from one body to another or simply, body jumping. Also, spirit migration can occur with inanimate objects, which are like holding cells until the host finds a suitable vessel. Lastly, there is a special migration that allows two souls to inhabit one body. But for that to work both hosts have to be in agreement or if the right requirements are met, unintentionally a migration can still take place."

"So you're telling me that my father's spirit is a stowaway in my friend Caleb's body?" Sophie asked disbelievingly.

"Well based on what you told me, it's a strong possibility that is the case. Obviously this friend of yours doesn't have any knowledge of your childhood nickname and certainly, it was not by chance that he called you, Kichona. So the only logical explanation based on the principles of re-pneuma, is that your father inhabits your friend's body. That means your friend came in contact with your father or with one of the items he blessed to house his spirit." replied the curator. Turning his back to Sophie, the curator asked, "How did your father die?" Taking a deep breath as tears welled up in her eyes, Sophie said, "The details of my father's death are unclear, but to make a long story short, my father was betrayed and murdered by his own crew." After hearing Sophie's brief account of her father's death, the curator puts the pieces together and deduces that her father's spirit is back to seek revenge for his betrayal and murder. And that somehow, Caleb was connected to her father. "Now, tell me about Caleb, what kind of person was he, before and after you noticed the tattoo?" asked the curator.

"Well, from the time I have known Caleb, he has always been a gentleman and very mild mannered. Now he's the opposite of that, he's aggressive and very nonchalant. And now that I'm thinking about it, he's been that way ever since we left the antique store. I remember, he was very upset that day and I convinced him to go for a walk and he opened up to me and shared how he caught his girlfriend, kissing another guy at work, who is a total jerk. Anyway he took me to this antique store and that's where I was reunited with my father's mirror. It was a happy occasion; I haven't seen that mirror in years—wait, that's when it had to have happened! I left him alone with the mirror, while I was purchasing it," exclaimed Sophie.

"Indeed, the right conditions. Your friend's anger for being betrayed by his girlfriend was the same as your father's betrayal by his crew. So Caleb was in direct contact with your father's mirror and I'm guessing that your father blessed that mirror as well. There you have it, all the necessary pieces for a perfect spirit transmigration. Your father is in your friend's body or at least sharing it. Now with that revelation, I must tell you your father's spirit won't rest until it gets its revenge and you should also be aware that a mirror reflection is an exact opposite of the image in front of it, so it's possible your friend Caleb, is trapped inside the mirror and a villainous mirror version of him is on the loose. If that's the case, then your friend's evil counterpart controls one portion of the time and your father's spirit controls the other portion," explained the curator. In disbelief of what she just heard, Sophie puts her hand on her head and flicks her hair back then asked "So what do I do now and how do I rescue Caleb?"

"Your father's spirit won't rest until he meets up with his killers and exacts his revenge. To rescue your friend, Caleb, you must first get the mirror version of him in front of your father's mirror and somehow get him back into the mirror. But this process has to be executed very quickly, if it's going to be successful. The two can't exist in the same world at the same time. Caleb will have to exit the mirror simultaneously as his evil counterpart enters the mirror or it won't work. The best way to save Caleb is to set a trap for the mirror version of him, but in order to do so, I imagine it would be best to know his whereabouts or, if you could track down the men that killed your father," exclaimed the curator.

CHAPTER: XX

The Agony of Revenge

Silenced by her frightening ability to comprehend and accept all the paranormal activities that surround her father and Caleb, Sophie jumps to her feet and shouted, "I know who he's going after!" Astonished by her forthcoming knowledge of the matter at hand, the curator exclaimed, "So, you know the men responsible for your father's death?"

"Not exactly, but I know the man who set him up. He's the father of another friend," answered Sophie.

"Another friend! Young lady this is no coincidence, that another friend of yours is involved in this triangle, this is the trinity of friends at work. Three kindred souls chosen before birth to be linked by great divine. You must get this other friend to help you, for he is the final piece to this puzzle and the one destined, along with yourself, to save your friend Caleb from the evil transgressions of the past," exclaimed the curator.

Meanwhile behind closed doors, a private meeting is about to take place, where a man in a suit prepares to meet with a dark man for a dark purpose. Upon entering the office, the man in the suit hands over an envelope and exclaimed. "Boss, I had the boys check around like you asked and nobody knows who hit "Respect." The only clues we found are in those photos, the message, "I'm back!" written in blood and the initials I.C. on the wall."

"Leave me!" exclaimed Gerard.

"But boss, those initials, to whom do they belong?" asked the man in the suit.

"I said leave me!" shouted Gerard. After the door closes, Gerard leans back in his chair and says, "So, you've returned, old friend." Then with his eyes closed, Gerard reminisces on days passed.

With the sound of a knock on the door, a voice answered, "Come in," then a rugged, able-bodied male walks inside wearing a black overcoat.

"Ian! What did I tell you about knocking?" asked Gerard.

"Not to," answered Ian.

"And yet you still do. So what's up; what can I do for you?" asked Gerard.

"Well... I've been doing some thinking about my life and I have decided it's time for me to retire," exclaimed Ian.

Pausing for a brief moment to puff his cigar, Gerard laughed. "Ok, you got me."

"Gerard, I'm serious. I want to do something different with my life, something meaningful," replied Ian.

With compassion in his voice Gerard said, "I know just how you feel. I too have often wondered what my life would be like, if I had chosen a different path. Or if I were born into a different family and had better opportunities afforded to me, but I have gotten over those feelings and so will you. Ian, take some time off, maybe go on vacation,"

Before Gerard could finish his statement, Ian shouted, "G, hear me out; I don't want or need time off; I'm done. I've made up my mind, I'm out and I hope you can understand?"

Sitting back in his chair with a disappointed look on his face, Gerard said, "You have obviously given this a lot of thought; you know things won't be the same without you. But since you feel so strongly about this, I'll make you a deal. One more job and that's it, you're out."

"One last job, no problem," Ian replied as he nodded his head.

Then in agreeance with the terms of the last job, Ian and Gerard shook hands, solidifying their bond as comrades, holding each other's forearm. After complying with Gerard's proposal, Ian excuses himself and takes his leave. Then, one of the other henchman asked, "Boss, are you really going to allow him leave?"

"Of course not, the only way out is in a box," snarled Gerard as he outed his cigar. Then reminiscing about the events of that fateful day, Gerard relives the

moment, when he stalked his battered prey and said, "Only way out is in a box," then pulled the trigger.

Sleeping soundly in bed as happy thoughts come to his mind, Belac also relives a moment in the past. *"Sophie come on, it's time to go, "said Ian.*

"But Dad, I'm having so much fun and you hardly ever take me to the park," exclaimed seven- year- old Sophie.

"I know, but Daddy has to go to work," replied Ian.

"You always have to go to work," pouted Sophie.

"I'm sorry, Kichona, but I have to go to work; it's a part of growing up. So your birthday is coming up this weekend, have you decided what you want?" asked Ian.

"Yes! Daddy, I want you to stay home, I don't want you to work no more. I want you to read me bedtime stories and pick me up after school. That's what I want, Daddy, no toys just you," replied Sophie as she hugged her father with tears in her eyes. Moved by his daughter's tears, Ian decided in his heart it's time to call it quits and become a devoted father to his daughter. After reliving that life-altering experience, Belac immediately opens his eyes and concludes it's time to visit his old friend.

Back at the theologian center, a car pulls up to the theological headquarters with the car horn blowing repeatedly. Darting towards the loud honking vehicle, Sophie runs to the sedan and enters it quickly. "Phillip, drive. We have to get to your father, he's in grave danger; I'll explain everything on the way," Sophie exclaimed."

With vengeance on the menu, Belac hides in the darkness of the night and scopes out, Legacy Auto mega car lot from a distance. While seeking retribution for the wrong done to him, Belac discovers a security detail of five armed men at the front gate and the face of an old acquaintance, the last of the three men who had a hand in his untimely demise. Aggressive by nature, fueled with revenge and righteous indignation, Belac decides to do what he does best and makes an entrance. In anticipation of the warning of a possible intruder, the security team stands guard at the front gate, waiting for any possible threat. Then suddenly, one member of the five-man security team catches sight of a speeding automobile advancing fiercely on their position. Alarmed by the quickly approaching vehicle, the security operative readies his weapon and shouted, "Hey, there's a blue automobile coming straight towards us!" Recognizing the blue Impala darting towards them, the head security said, "Stand down! That's just the boss overly sensitive son; it's just another one of his temper tantrums, crazy kid, he's no threat, just a disappointment. He'll stop in front of the gate, just like last time." As the vehicle gets closer, another operative screamed, "He's not stopping! Get out of the way!" Bam! Belac slams through the gate and takes out three members of the security details in one fell swoop.

After causing a calamity at the front gate, Belac exits the wrecked vehicle and produces a 9mm handgun and discharges three shots into the abdomen of the fourth security operative. With his assailant's back turned to him, the head security operative struggles to his feet, having injured his leg while jumping out of harm's way. Taking advantage of Belac unawareness of his presence, the security operative seizes the moment and shoots Belac in the shoulder. Afflicted by a graze wound, Belac drops his gun as the head security operative draws closer to him with his gun pointed; now the hunter had become the hunted. Fixated on his attacker, the head security operative hobbles closer to Belac, ready to put an end to him, but before he could carry out his fiendish plan, Belac drops to the ground and shoots the head security operative in the neck and chest with his other acquired firearm, a .38 special magnum.

Cautiously getting back on his feet, Belac checks his surroundings then enters the establishment. After entering the building, Belac searches the premises in hopes of locating Gerard, but instead of finding the man he once regarded as a comrade, his explorations lead him to an old acquaintance. As the two men engage in a standoff, the henchman looks at Belac and exclaimed, "Anyone can win a gun battle but a real man uses his fists to prove his dominance." Then in agreeance, both men throw down their weapons and commenced in an all-out brawl; but when it is all said and done, Belac is the victor. Continuing his relentless hunt for Gerard, Belac feels a slight stiffness in his shoulder as the damages sustained during the fight and the graze wound begin to take effect on his body as he picked up his gun and limps away.

Continuing his manhunt, Belac checks behind every door looking for his one-time boss. Then at last his search comes to an end as Belac opens the last door and finally comes face to face with the man he admired, trusted and worked with, the man who took everything away from him, including his life. Sitting in his chair, calmly enjoying a drink, Gerard looks at Belac and said, "You came back, just like you said you would." Then thinking back to that fateful day, both men recalled their last meeting together, when Ian drew his last breaths and stuttered, *"Abba, please preserve my soul that I may be reborn, so I can right the wrong done to me...I'll be back."* After conjuring up memories from the past, Belac points his gun and said, "Good, you remembered. I don't have to explain why I'm here."

"No you don't," answered Gerard boldly, then making a final request Gerard said, "Before we get down to business, please have a drink with me and allow me to at least explain my actions."

"Ok, one drink," exclaimed Belac.

Rising from his chair, Gerard goes to his cocktail cabinet and pours two glasses of whiskey, refilling one glass for himself and the other for Belac with something extra added in it. Then walking over to Belac, Gerard hands over the glass and said, "To old friends, may we learn from our mistakes." With the toast given, Belac proceeds to consume his drink, as Gerard watches carefully. With wicked glee, Gerard consumes his drink slowly, highly pleased that he had Belac, snared into his fatal trap. Then a gunshot is discharged, and his glass drops and shatters as his body hits the floor. Covered in blood, staring down the barrel of a chrome Beretta, Ian exclaimed, "I learned from my mistake and trusting you was mine; you honestly thought I was going to trust taking a drink from the likes of you? You were always a coward, back then and now; that's why you sent them first to do your dirty work, then you came in after to pick up the pieces. You know only a true coward resorts to poison. You were always sneaky, that's why your plan failed and things ended differently. I saw you taking your time pouring those drinks. I knew you were up to no good, so I made a plan of my own, I pretended to drink that whiskey just like you wanted. And when I saw that your guard was down and you were lulled into a false sense of security, I knew it was time and pulled the trigger. Life is full of ironies, I was going to finish you with this magnum but after seeing your gun drop, I knew it was fate. Now your famous words will haunt you "Only way out is in a box." Then seven thunderous shots echoed. Moments later, after the massacre, Phillip and Sophie arrive at Legacy Auto, to warn Phillip's father about the impending danger coming to claim his life. But upon their arrival they realized that they were are too late as they found a pathway of death, carnage and destruction leading to Gerard's lifeless body.

CHAPTER: XXI

The Trap

The next day, Belac wakes up feeling accomplished as he walks into the bathroom to wash his face. Looking into the mirror, Ian said, "The atonement for the wrong done to me is complete and it's time for us to return, so I can finally be at rest." In response to Ian's declaration, Belac replied, "I'm not going back and you can't make me; and besides, I like it out here."

"I can't make you? You forget who's in control, when you are asleep," exclaimed Ian. Then pausing for a moment Belac said. "I didn't forget. But what you fail to remember is that I now have the advantage and before you get any bright ideas, I'm going to destroy that mirror, then I'm going to kill Eric and have some fun. Now if you'll excuse me, I have a big day ahead of me."

Meanwhile at Phillip's apartment, Sophie spends the night to comfort Phillip on the loss of his father. "Phillip, I know how hard it is to lose your dad; believe me, I know how that feels but right now you have to pull yourself together for Caleb. We still have to rescue him and get the evil Caleb back into the mirror," exclaimed Sophie.

"You're right. Let's focus on rescuing Caleb," replied Phillip, "So based on what you have told me, we need to set a trap in order to catch the evil Caleb, but the question is how?" After a few minutes of pondering and coming up with nonsensical plans, Sophie shouts, "I've got it! We'll use bait to trap him and who is the one person in the world, both Caleb's dislike?" then like a beautifully sung duet both Phillip and Sophie shout simultaneously, "Eric!"

Now in the process of carrying out his sinister plan to stay in this world and assume Caleb's identity, Belac visits the antique store, where it all began. Upon entering the store, Belac wastes no time and walks right up to the store clerk and said, "I'm looking for a mirror."

"Sir, you came to the right place, we have many different types of mirrors for you to choose from. We have small mirrors, we have round mirrors, we have metallic mirrors and we even have vintage mirrors."

"No, I'm looking for the large wall size mirror with a golden frame, you had in the display window," exclaimed Belac.

"Unfortunately, that particular mirror was sold to a young lady last week," answered the clerk.

"I must have that mirror. Please give me that young lady's name and address, so I can talk with her," Belac pleaded.

"I'm sorry but I can't give you that information, it's against store policy. Perhaps you would be interested in another mirror?" replied the clerk.

Annoyed with the clerk's refusal to provide him with the necessary information required to locate the mirror, Belac squints his eyes as he looks at the clerk, then taking out a pocket knife, Belac stabs the clerk in his hand, pinning it to the counter. Continuing his interrogation Belac turns the knife slowly and promises the clerk, that if he told him who the young lady is, who bought the mirror and gives him her address, he would end his suffering. Unable to bear, the excruciating pain of a steel blade slowly tearing through his flesh, the clerk gives up and screamed, "Ok! Her name is Sophie and this is the address where we delivered the mirror." Keeping his end of the bargain, Belac withdraws the knife out of the clerk's hand and quickly stabs him in the neck then sets out with his new plan to confront Eric and find Sophie.

Moments later, just outside Global Media as Eric was about to report in for duty, Phillip and Sophie pull up in a red sedan and urge Eric to come with them. While trying to convince Eric that his life is in danger and that he needed to come with them, here comes Belac shows up from behind the building. Immediately laying eyes on Eric, Belac takes out his knife and goes berserk as he runs menacingly towards Eric, screaming his name. In total fear for his life, Eric quickly dashes into the vehicle and shouted repeatedly, "Go, go, go!" With the pedal to the metal, Phillip speeds off like a racecar driver leaving Belac to smell fumes as they drive off to Sophie's home. Rather than being angry that his plan to mutilate Eric was foiled, Belac seizes the moment and says to himself, "*I love it, when a plan comes together,*" then continues his pursuit.

A short time later a taxi cab pulls up and Belac steps out and declared his intentions, "Phillip...Sophie, I mean you no harm, you two are my friends. I just want Eric and the mirror, so don't get in my way. " With the proclamation of his demands, Belac kicks open the front door and enter Sophie's home. Looking around, Belac says in a loud voice, "Ready or not, here I come. Eric, you and I have history and this was a long time coming. I believe they call it destiny. Phil, I know you must be upset, but I didn't kill your father, you have to believe me. Sophie, don't be afraid; you know I would never hurt you, I only want the mirror."

After making his decree, Belac walks through the front door of Sophie's home and begins his search for the mystic mirror and his prey. About halfway into the hallway, Eric reveals himself to Belac. As their eyes meet, Eric begins making amends for all the wrong he did to Caleb, seeking forgiveness. But with a fiendish smirk on his face, Belac said, "Your death is the only atonement, I seek." Withdrawing his knife, Belac walks slowly towards Eric and exclaimed, "This won't take long." While making a beeline towards Eric, Belac is oblivious to Phillip sneaking up behind him. Filled with fear, Eric begins walking backwards and accidently drags down the sheet covering the mirror in his haste to escape, causing Phillip's reflection to be seen.

With lightning fast reflexes, Belac turns around and stabs Phillip in the stomach. Emotional after witnessing Belac's knife, entering and exiting Phillip's torso, Sophie leaves her hiding spot filled with rage and charges full speed at Belac. Unable to dash Belac to the ground, Sophie jumps onto Belac's back and bites him on the shoulder to stop him from further injuring Phillip. While Belac struggles to get Sophie off his back, Phillip catches a break as his body crashes to the floor. Partially immobile because of his wound, Phillip somehow finds the strength and crawls slowly towards the mirror and yells for Caleb.

As Belac continues his uphill battle with Sophie, glimpses of Caleb can be seen, each time Belac moves in view of the mirror. Observing the flickers of Caleb's reflection in the mirror, Phillip screamed, "Caleb, when the evil you get close to the mirror, you have to pull him in and jump out quickly, or you will be stuck in there forever!" Suddenly in the midst of their struggle, Belac slams himself against the wall, knocking Sophie out and freeing himself of her chokehold. Turning his attention to the mirror, Belac runs fiercely towards the mystic mirror, in all hopes of destroying it but his plan was disrupted once again as Phillip throws himself in the way and saves the mirror from being demolished. Infuriated with yet another one of his plans being interfered with, Belac mercilessly beats down the wounded Phillip until he was unable to withstand any more blows. As Phillip's body hits the floor, Belac and

Caleb at long last, finally meet face to face once again, then Belac exclaimed, "I'm sorry, Caleb... but I'm permanently working this side of the mirror."

Just then, as all seemed lost, help from an unexpected ally comes to the rescue in the form of Eric, as he strikes Belac in the back of his head with a vase. What seemed to be a game changer, only manages to anger Belac even more as the attack wasn't enough even to slow him down. Turning to Eric, Belac attempts to carry out his objective, which was to execute Eric, but once again, Phillip manages to hinder Belac's plan as he grabs hold of Belac's leg, preventing him from achieving his goal. At that same time awakening from her K.O. status, Sophie catches hold of the situation and quickly springs into action. Dashing Belac into the mirror, Sophie screamed, "Caleb now!" With the support and determination of his friends risking all to rescue him, Caleb musters the strength and reaches for Belac and pulls him into the mirror. While pulling Belac into the mirror, Caleb attempts to jump out simultaneously, but Belac latches onto Caleb's foot and prevents him from escaping the mirror. With half of Caleb's body out of the mirror, Eric and Sophie each grab a hand and try to help pull Caleb out of the mirror, but Belac refuses to give up. Then in the midst of the tug of war, Eric screamed, "Caleb, kick him off!" Without a second thought Caleb takes the advice of Eric and begins kicking Belac. After being kicked multiple times, Belac starts to lose his grip as the struggle of pulling against Eric and Sophie wears him down. Then like shattered glass, Belac's grip is broken and at long last Caleb is finally freed from the mirror.

Epilogue

After surviving the onslaught of Caleb's evil mirror double Belac, our heroes close this terrifying chapter in their lives with the destruction of the mirror and the sealing of Belac.

With the sinister mirror double Belac back where he belonged and new hopes arising, Caleb, Eric, Phillip and Sophie all embark on their new journeys as they embrace their destinies.

Eric started a new career in timeshare as a salesman, after being fired for his confession of stealing Caleb's portfolio.

Phillip took over his father's business, after leaving Global Media and created a new legacy, one of hope, nobility and integrity.

Caleb finally got the promotion that he desired and worked for, along with the respect due to him.

And as for Sophie, she got her heart's desire: a place in Caleb's heart and his life.

Caleb and Sophie months later:

Enjoying all the happiness that life could offer being in a relationship, Caleb and Sophie take a trip out of town to commemorate their six-month anniversary. After spending a perfect weekend together, the newly formed couple enjoyed their last night celebrating to the very end. Awakening the next morning from his slumber, Caleb rolls out of bed and smiles as he watches Sophie sleep. Moving closer to her, Caleb leans over and kisses Sophie on the forehead then makes his way to the bathroom. While washing his face, Caleb unsuspectingly falls victim to the constructs of his mind as he stares into the mirror on the bathroom wall. Brought back to reality by the shock of feeling two arms wrapping around his waist, Caleb pitches forward as he is startled by Sophie, who sneaks up behind him to give him a hug.

"What's wrong?" asked Sophie.

Taking a breath Caleb exclaimed, "I was back in there it felt so…," but before Caleb could finish his sentence, Sophie puts her finger on his lips and exclaimed, "Shhh, This is real, now go in the shower."

Without hesitation, Caleb quickly gets undressed and steps into the shower. Teasing Caleb, Sophie seductively disrobes then proceeds to freshen up. After cleansing her face Sophie looks into the mirror and there, right before her very eyes stood Belac. With her eyes wide, Sophie glances at Caleb in the shower then back at Belac as he said, "You know what you have to do."

TO BE CONTINUED...

Made in the USA
Middletown, DE
23 July 2018